LIFE IN A FACELESS WORLD

Based on the lost and found diary
of a girl named Nila

CYRIL MUKALEL

POTTER'S WHEEL PUBLISHING HOUSE
MINNEAPOLIS

LIFE IN A FACELESS WORLD by CYRIL MUKALEL

Published by POTTER'S WHEEL PUBLISHING HOUSE
MINNEAPOLIS
MN 55378

www.POTTERSWHEELPUBLISHING.com

© 2019 CYRIL MUKALEL

For permissions contact:
info@POTTERSWHEELPUBLISHING.com

Cover by Maduranga Nuwan
Book layout and design by Sarco Press

ISBN-13: 978-1-950399-00-0
ISBN-10: 1-950399-00-1
LCCN: 2019934996

To my Father and Mother
who began to dream of me becoming an author
from the moment I was born

Acknowledgement

Journey through the faceless world was an incredible experience. I was never alone; many faces and their unheard voices were by my side; trying to tell me something. There are many who helped and encouraged me to stay focused on completing this book. Though it is hard to acknowledge everyone in this limited space, I at least want to mention a few who made significant contributions in this humble attempt.

I am grateful to Robert Farid Karimi who guided and taught me the craft of storytelling. You shined my strength and helped me to overcome my flaws.

Growing up in the setting of "God of Small Things" and experiencing it, instilled an urge in me to author a book. I am obliged to its amazing creator Arundhati Roy.

My sincere gratitude to Loft Literary Center and the Inroads fellowship program that helped me to build a strong foundation as a writer. It was a blessing to be enlightened in imagination along with fellow scholars Nimo Farah, Lillian Brion, Eva Song Margolis, Rebecca Chung, Luis M. Lopez, and Rebecca Song.

I would especially like to thank India Association of Minnesota (IAM,) The Indic Foundation and Dr. Dash Foundation for their ongoing support and encouragement to writers/artists like me and our works.

A special thanks to my editors. Kellie Wynn for her sincerity and for caring so deeply about my work, and Paul Ryan for his keen sense and talent to achieve the right level of perfection.

Maduranga Nuwan for the brilliant Cover page and Glenn at

Sarco Press for making every page in this book flow smooth and perfect.

I can never adequately thank Kavitha my wife, and our children Anjali, Ashwin, and Alan who were my first readers and best critiques.

I want to thank my older brother Jossy for challenging me to accomplish something unexpected of me in life, and my sister Asha who symbolizes unconditional love and affection. My younger siblings Rajesh and Sonia who blindly support and cheer me in whatever I attempt.

My sincere thanks to the critics and beta readers who helped me to perfect and feel confident of my work. John Gardiner, Stella Jacob, Dr. Richard Zelonka, Radhika Bhadran, Jayesh Naithani, Mohan Kannan, Terry Hayne, Cynthia Parten, Lucy Paulose, Godan Namboothiripad, Brian Williams, Sunitha Vijay and Ron Palmer, Jagan Muttasseril, Alex Cherucheril, Jais Kannachan and many others.

And to all my readers, without you all my hard work is pointless. You bring the characters in this book to life and give them an adequate place in this world.

Contents

Foreword ix

Arranged Marriage 3

The Telescope 11

Hero & Heroine 21

Life in a Faceless World 49

Dreams 73

Neelan (The Blue Man) 97

Farmer's Market 113

Dr. Thomas Ape 143

SWAMI (The Holy Man) 153

Living among the Life Savers 167

    Apparition 169

    Raising the Dead 175

    Snakes and Ladder 179

    Rose Garden 183

    Precious Moments 187

Who is Nila? 195

Beacons of Light 199

Foreword

LIVING AMONG PEOPLE of varied backgrounds, traditions, and heritages has sparked an ardent interest in me to promote oneness. To be a part of the beacon, I chose to tap into both my imagination and my writing skills. The principles and dreams of ordinary people have been a huge influence in shaping my values and goals. The focus of my writing is to promote a greater understanding between cultures and to facilitate a friendship between diverse groups—thereby removing the fences that divide us. As a writer with experience in both the western and eastern worlds, I believe it is my responsibility, not simply my passion, to complete this book. Each chapter of this book is presented as an expansion of the contents and events relating to a "lost and found" diary of the protagonist. This fiction depicts the life of Nila, a young woman from South Asia, who had to relocate to the United States due to an arranged marriage. Cultural life and the mindset of people from this region are unfamiliar to the western world; the story of her life and the world around her is virtually untold. As the matrix of color and cultural combinations change in our society, it is essential that integration occurs and breaks down the barriers of differences. This is my humble attempt to introduce readers to unique and interesting characteristics of the diverse lifestyles of people to facilitate awareness and amity.

Nila grew up in a culture different from the one she wanted to assimilate into. Through her eyes, I attempt to paint the dreams and mismatched realities of life using the colors of both joy and sorrow. Each story detailed in this book is extremely relevant; each exposes the challenges and realities faced and the unique, yet unheard, voices of people around us.

If you are looking in these pages for the life of Nila

You may not find anything more than what I have learned

The story of Nila is the story of many... the ones who touched her life

...their sorrows and joy, adventures, and losses, but above all

It holds the secret to finding true happiness in the midst of struggles in our lives

16 MAY

A boy is coming to see me. Hope he is the one...

We were travelers on paths that never met,
But we were always meant to be.
When the jasmines held their breath
Stars told us we were always meant to be.

Charcoal figures we drew over these walls
left the village searching for the new pastures.
A lone cloud far from its pack longs for a breeze,
to reach where it is meant to be.
Paintball splashed on an autumn sky,
Disgraced king waits in a clown's costume.
People I thought knew me well left early.
Is this what conviction is meant to be?

Silence of the forest holds its breath
Dead saint with a pale halo over his head.
Soon the last petal drifts away; it is no more a flower.
The way life's realities are meant to be

Paper boats in this puddle carry our shadows
They avoid the rain drops to stay afloat.
Colorless images make vivid memories.
Your lips shut your eyes dream as meant to be.

Somewhere inside the hardest stone,
you can still hear its tears groan.
Seed in the swamp where sunlight never let it sprout
and it knows that is meant to be.

Spiraling colors slip through deceptive eyes
Windows shut the house gasps.
Let us go into the forest, brine of our love
The home where we always meant to be.

Arranged Marriage

NILA NEVER THOUGHT the night could be this long. The silence of the night and the darkness filled the room, making her uncomfortable. She stretched her arm out as far as possible to touch her sister. Her little sister, Anu, was sound asleep under her favorite green cashmere blanket on the floor beside her bed. The sound of the pendulum on the wall clock seemed to have slowed down quite a bit. Maybe Appa, her dad, had forgotten to wind it last Sunday. The clock always reminded her of Appa, as Amma, her mother joked about him saying,

"Your Appa is like a clock. Always busy running around and talking, either to himself or to someone else." Restlessly, she kept twisting and turning hoping to see a tiny grin of light through the crack of the wooden window. It was always shut to keep the mosquitoes away.

The moment she heard the rooster crowing to announce the night has ended, Nila swiftly flung the blanket off and sprang out of her bed. Carefully, without waking anyone else, she tiptoed into the living room. Then quietly, she removed the latches to open the front split doors and stepped onto the veranda. The freshness of the crisp morning air, scented in jasmine, made her feel she was still in a dream. Large shoe flowers had bloomed in the night and covered all its branches, and the leaves were red velvet. The dew drops strewn all over had turned into reddish gems.

"Wow! A big green grasshopper on the pillar! This should be my lucky day."

She stepped into the flip-flops lying on the steps, jumped out into the front yard, and walked toward the cow shed over on the south side of the courtyard.

"Good morning, Lakshmi!"

Lakshmi twitched her ears and stretched her head, then swung her tongue as if she wanted to lick Nila's hand. She massaged her forehead and played with her tiny horns. With her dark brown eyes and the softest skin, Nila thought Lakshmi was the most beautiful cow in the world. The black beauty spot on her golden-skinned face made her look even more beautiful than *Kamadenu,* the divine cow that grants all the wishes of its owner. She thought if Lakshmi were a real girl, she would be the most beautiful girl, probably better looking than Aishwarya Rai, the best-looking one in the world. She walked slowly to the chicken cage, looking for the eggs, lifting each sleepy hen and placing them carefully in the small, round reed basket stored under the cage roof. With the basket, she walked over the cobblestones that separated the courtyard from the cattle shed.

"Hey girl… be careful, don't jump around and sprain your ankle. They are coming today to see you." Her mother reminded her from the kitchen window in a rather anxious but jovial tone.

"If they really like me, they shouldn't care if my leg is sprained or broken, Amma." She replied with the guts of an insolent young woman.

"You naughty one, don't display your silliness before them. They may think you are crazy. If you don't get married before you turn twenty-two, you will have to wait another thirteen years to pass the Saturn," her mom reminded. Of course she couldn't forget about the warning given by the family astrologist who saw complications to her marriage prospects based on her horoscope.

"Amma, I don't care, I will stay single if I don't find the right man and don't care for the horoscope." It angered Nila.

"Nila, don't forget your parents won't be here forever to take care of you. We are getting old." Nila ignored her mother who tried to add some emotional blackmail to the conversation.

The parrot in the cage hanging outside the kitchen on the tip of the rafter kept saying, "Nila, be careful."

On her way back up the steps, she angrily looked at the parrot and screamed, "Shut up!" and it echoed her "Chut-up. Chut-up." Nila laughed loud and placed the egg basket on the half wall close to the pillar that surrounded the portico. With her left hand around the pillar, she swung herself over the steps and into the portico. She turned around and looked at the misty hill behind the rice fields which sat in front of her house. The round black rock, covered with dry moss on the hill with dark green grass around it, looked like a giant eye on the hill. She thought the hill laughed with her and those eyes welled up when she was sad.

The magnificent cloud layers that switched colors every moment stole her mind, and they painted her dreams yet to be unleashed. With her eyes glued to it and with her golden anklets chiming to the rhythms budding in her heart, she walked back and sat on the wooden long-armed chair placed over the portico. She always loved to sit on the huge majestic chair, made with rosewood that was passed onto her Appa from his father, a symbol of power and heritage passed down from generation to generation. Sitting there, Nila felt she controlled everything she could see, including the hill that boarded their property and the clouds over it. Appa didn't like anyone else sitting on it and reminded everyone to stay away. He claimed it was the symbol of the authority his forefathers were given from the *Chola* King, who designated them as his deputies in this land after the war between *Chera* and the *Chola* kingdoms. The first thing her Appa did after he woke up was to sit on the chair for an hour and read the newspaper from one end to the other. She wished for Appa to sleep for another hour and delay the exercise of his imaginary power over the relics of the lost kingdom from the past dreams.

She looked at the beautiful world in front of her and waited for the picturesque sunrise. The paddy field in front of her stretched out over twenty acres. Its other end reached close to the foot of the hill. Her little brother, Arun, thought the sun waited behind that hill till morning to rise. He always wanted to get up early, go to the hill and see the hiding sun, but he could never wake up that early. The green-carpeted field turned gold with the ripening rice flowers weaving golden thread over it. The clouds above the hill looked magnificent, like a masterpiece painting with each color competing with one another to look better. Two sparrows flew close to her and said something to each other, and then disappeared into the paddy fields. Although they sounded like Appa and Amma quarreling, she wondered if they were exchanging their love for each other. Nila felt the chill of the morning breeze hugging her; it gave her goosebumps all over.

Nila went to her room quietly without waking up her sister, opened her trunk box, and took out her black diary. Holding it close to her chest she walked swiftly to the armchair, opened the outer cover and removed the black and white photograph which was hidden in its sleeve pocket. She looked at the face in the photo and tried to replace the hero in her daydreams with the one in the picture. His smile and the innocence on his face was what made her fall in love with him right away, even before seeing him.

"This is the fourth person coming to see me. I feel… this is the one." Her intuition overcame her worries. She needed to feel positive about the whole ordeal about the arranged marriage, and the visit of men to see their potential bride. It was not her superstition, but her previous experiences that had taught her success can come only after three failures. When the first man who had a job in Saudi Arabia came to see her, he liked the rice field and the hill behind it more than he liked her. He was more interested in finding its real estate worth if sold so as to take advantage of the booming tourism industry. The other two were not much different from each other. They looked somewhat creepy to her, had no opinion about anything, and behaved like boys that always clung to their mom's *sari*.

Without being aware, she found her mind was dancing with the waving golden rice flowers in the first rays of the rising sun. While her eyes kept staring at the photo, she drifted with the gentle morning breeze to dissolve herself into a sweet, charming melody that engrossed her.

"Nila, are you done sleeping this early? Get me a coffee."

"OK, Appa." She stood up instantly upon seeing her dad and ran inside with the diary.

"Nila..."

She turned back.

Her dad picked up the photo from the floor, where it must have fallen in her haste to get up, gave it to her and said, "Keep it safe, incase this doesn't work out, we have to return it back to the marriage broker." While she went inside, the parrot kept saying "Nila be careful, Nila be careful." Blushing, she looked at the teasing parrot and winked at it with a bashful grin, then ran to the kitchen.

At the apartment parking lot,
a girl came running to us.
She was crying. She wanted to
say something

I walk on footprints
Measuring their depth
Some get deeper and deeper
As if the weight they carried
Mounted with every step.
Footprints have taken me to places
No one ever would dare to go
I know they would
Never look into your eye
Their feet never talk to their mind.
I've seen footprints crisscrossing themselves
I never wanted to find why.
Some stop in the middle of nowhere
It worries me; I look around
I listen for their murmurs, their cries
Cracked shells under my trapped feet squeal in pain.
Some days I get lost in footprints
I panic. Sultry sea breeze makes me sweat
I look away and walk towards the vanishing sun
Feathery waves wash my mind
Making my feet light as before
I walk away from the footprints
But they keep following me.

The Telescope

THE PHONE BROKE the silence, waking Nila from her drifting daydreams. She grabbed the phone before the second ring. "Hello?"

"Hey, Nila, sorry, but I'm going to be late. There's a production issue at the office. Let's go out tomorrow...Ok?"

"Ashok, it's Friday, you've two days to fix the problems. I am tired of sitting alone in this tiny apartment."

"Sorry... sweetie... This is a major computer system. The whole country uses it. I got to go, Bye!"

"Ba...yee."

Nila almost cried. She turned the phone off and threw herself into the couch, angrily beating herself on the forehead. As usual, she complained to her favorite god, Lord Krishna's statue on the TV top.

"I tell him all the time to move out of this place to a better one. He never listens, just blames his H1 Work Visa. Oh... I forgot, why am I telling you all this? Your eardrums must be bursting after listening to those sixteen thousand whining wives of yours."

After turning the TV on and off few times impatiently with the clicker, Nila rose and slowly walked to the window. She opened the blinds by pulling the string on the side like the curtain before the show.

"Ladies and gentlemen, welcome to Nila's World!" the lonely extrovert announced sarcastically. The apartment's wide living room window faced the always-busy Pennsylvania Avenue, which in turn made her feel she was in a crowd; a crowd that kept her busy all the time.

"Oh no! The whole window's covered with moisture. Maybe my cooking without running the exhaust fan is causing this."

She looked through the hazy window at the cars entering the parking lot. The bump at the entrance made the cars bounce. Headlights made shadows of the naked tree branches like alien figures on the moist window. With her index finger, she drew a smiley face with long hair and a dot on the forehead between her eyebrows. Beneath the drawing, she signed her name 'Nila Ashok.' Giggling, she went to the kitchen to grab a paper towel. She wiped away her name, then cleaned, in circles, the whole window.

"Wow! Look at you, moon. You look so pretty tonight! You seem to like the fall and the snow better than summer, right?

Hey Cinderella of the skies, I am going to give you company the whole night. You might be wondering why I am all alone on this Friday evening. You know Ashok, right? Do you want me to tell you more? He and his job... you know... his company will shut down without him working there." She kept laughing. The moon, as if to tease her, disappeared behind a piece of a cloud for a few moments.

Nila opened the window by turning the crank handle a bit. Cool air rushed through the opening to embrace her.

"It feels so good."

Nila breathed in the cool air. The chill made goosebumps ripple all over her. Without taking her eye from the captivating full moon, she stepped back and stood behind the telescope placed near the center pane. She adjusted the tripod and wiped the surface of the blue *Orion* telescope, a gift from Ashok on her twenty-third birthday. What could be a better gift for someone who lives in dreams the whole day, letting the mind wander with the stars and the clouds? The telescope kept her busy making friends with the stars and the moon. She engaged in long conversations, sharing her little fantasies and little sorrows of boredom with them.

Parrot that is what Ashok called her when she forgets to halt her chatterbox. Whenever Ashok was late from work, Nila journeyed into the unexplored universe, dissolving into its mysteries. She looked for the newborn stars and plotted them into her notebook connecting stars to form different figures and shapes she loved. She identified the stars by referring to the *Astronomer's Pocket Guide;* then named the newly found ones with her friends' names. She logged stories of her encounters in the diary, hiding behind the cursive revelations.

While taking a break from her discoveries of unknown truths of the skies, Nila humbled herself by looking down into the lives of earthly dwellers. She gazed at the people walking along the busy Pennsylvania Avenue and could easily recognize almost everyone there. To identify them, she gave them fictitious names from Greek mythology and Ramayana. She envisioned wars between the Greek Gods and the Monkey Forces from Ramayana in the busy street and the apartment parking lot.

Nila spied on everyone who passed through the territory under her control.

Successfully, she predicted who would come to the street next and knew what bus they would take. When she looked in the bathroom mirror, she imitated them and mimicked their mannerisms. When people were absent for few days or displayed bad temper for an extended period, she grew really concerned.

With constant practice, she gained the skill to move the telescope quickly to identify faces in fast-moving cars. *Is this a skill or an addiction, not leaving anyone alone, and invading the privacy of their minds?* She thought with remorse, then shelved it. Reading minds and predicting their future with her telescope became part of her routine. On weekends, she tried to hide her obsession but at times instinctively touched the telescope focused to the street. Ashok never noticed or at least acted as if he didn't; maybe he wanted her to be busy when he became deeply engrossed in his spaghetti of software code. He believed, without him nurturing the system, the company would be in deep trouble. Literally, he even took the water cooler jokes aimed at him way too seriously. "Ashok, if you're hit by a truck or a train, our jobs and the company will be in serious trouble." So he avoided driving his Toyota Corolla near big trucks and was cautious at the railroad crossings.

Nila pointed the telescope at the sky and focused on a distant star. Her mind drifted through memory lane. Her eyes quickly turned soggy and she saw no stars or the planets. But then one star started glowing more and more every moment she looked at it. It had been a while since she enjoyed the brightness of the moon, rings around Saturn, or the beauty spots of Jupiter with her telescope. Every time she looked through the eyepiece, she saw only one face—the face of her friend Shahana. The pretty face that came through her telescope lens like a meteor… then disappeared after spreading few glimpses of happiness in her life.

It was during one of those parking lot spy missions, Nila was overwhelmed in surprise to see someone like herself. She zeroed in on the starlit-eyed, beautiful girl with a teeny touch of gloom on her face. She was wearing a purple headscarf with scattered red roses embroidered on it. Nila quickly ran down the stairs to the parking lot, but the girl had disappeared.

WEEKS PASSED BY and still Nila kept looking for the girl she saw through the telescope. At last, Nila's search fruited in the congestion of the noisy laundry room where she met Shahana for the first-time face to face. The pungent smell of bleach and the leftover detergent powder smudges did not impede her excitement. She felt like she was seeing her long-lost best friend after a very long break.

The delight of finding a friend by surprise at a time engrossed in solitude, made Nila talkative, nervous, and scrambling for words. The smile and the unfamiliarity in a world of familiarity turned into thick friendship in moments. Shahana hardly spoke English. She went to school until fourth grade in her hometown in Bangladesh where the elders forbade girls studying further. Thanks to all the Hindi movies they both watched prior to coming to the US, they had a few words in common that came in handy. They created a perfect communication complete with smiles, laughs, and gestures mixed with the scarce words of English they knew.

They met every day in the laundry room, where as the machines removed dirt from the clothes, they relieved their sorrows. As days passed by, when the last snow on the ground melted away, they took their friendship outside the building. They spent time in the park and walked in the street. For hours, they sat at the bus stop as if they were waiting for a bus to a journey that would never end. The right bus never came to pick them up, nor did they stop waiting. They wandered around the apartment buildings. Nila laughed and talked way more than Shahana could listen. She just kept smiling while hiding all her pain under the colorful scarf on her head.

Despite Nila's compelling attempts to invite Shahana to visit her apartment, she never showed up. She just kept smiling at her invitation. Nila was not sure what this meant but was always hopeful. Whenever she asked about her husband, Shahana just ignored the question and kept quiet. During the last conversation, she noticed Shahana's eyes tearing up with the mention of her husband. She asked nothing more about him after that incident.

Some days later, Nila was testing her newly acquired embroidery skills, when she heard a sudden knock on the door. She got a little nervous, quickly stopped working, then walked to the door. Through the peephole, she looked, then screamed in joy.

"Shaha…" She fumbled with the chain lock and opened the door.

"At last, you came to my home!" She pulled Shahana in.

Shahana tried to smile, but the sadness overpowered her. She hugged Nila and cried. She wept for a long time, holding Nila tightly. Nila heard footsteps in the hallway coming closer. She patted Shahana's shoulder and closed the door with the other hand. They walked into the living room.

"Sit, Shahana. Is everything OK?"

Her friend kept crying, the tears rolling down her cheeks. Nila didn't know what to do, but to cry with her. She couldn't control herself, wiping tears with the tip of her sari; she grabbed few tissues, and gave them to Shahana.

Shahana removed her headscarf. Nila saw the red eyes and the marks all over her face.

"Oh no!" She looked closely and felt with her fingers the face blackened by beatings, and the burns from a cigarette.

"What happened, Shahana?" she cried. "Sameer… he beat me up and tried to kill me."

SAMEER, HER HUSBAND, was a butcher at the international market store. He cut and cleaned fish from morning to close. Some days he didn't come home. One of her friends said he had another woman near his work, and wasted all his money gambling. Shahana unloaded all her pain and shared her grief with her best friend.

Nila applied Neosporin ointment and stuck Band-Aids over the marks. She tied the scarf for her.

"You are so beautiful, Shahana! Merciful Allah will make him good. I will pray for you both." Smiling, Shahana left to go to her apartment.

On a Sunday just before Christmas, Nila saw her for the last time. Shahana was going somewhere with her husband. Prior to getting into the car, she looked back and waved in the direction of Nila's apartment. Nila didn't know if she could see her or not but thought everything had changed for the better.

After that day, Nila never saw her in the laundry room or elsewhere. Being extremely concerned, she thought of going alone to check on her in their apartment.

Maybe I will go with Ashok when he comes home. That won't be a good idea, I will have to tell him everything, and he may get mad at me. Her wavering mind didn't let her make any decision, but it was slowly transforming her into a person that she could never be.

It was midnight, Nila and Ashok jumped out of the bed, ran to the window to look at the police siren and ambulance. The fire truck was parked with lights flashing near the street. They watched from their bedroom window as a stretcher with a body covered in a cloth was brought near the ambulance. Nila's heart stopped, and her body became paralyzed when she saw Sameer walking behind the police officer. He had the facial expression of a hungry clown. It was hard to make out if he was laughing or crying.

"Shah—" Hysterically, Nila ran and pushed opened the balcony's sliding door.

"What's wrong, Nila? You know them? Why don't you go to bed? Everything will be all right." Ashok rubbed her back to calm her down. Silently, she walked to the living room, looked through the telescope at the street. The ambulance and the police car went away, flashing its lights. The next day while she searched through the galaxies, Nila saw a new star among the familiar ones. It was staring at her and was beautiful like her friend. She named it Shahana.

~

IT IS ALMOST a year since a full moon like this took Nila's friend away. Time was racing faster than ever, storing precious moments with foggy memories. She focused the telescope on Shahana and began her never-ending chatter, forgetting everything around her.

Excited!

At last... visit Auntie Molly for the first time after coming to the US

Some thoughts come to us for no reason
It makes figures before us
They are reflections
We hold its arms and dance to the dying tunes
Under the blinding strobe lights, our eyes begin to melt
We are lovers holding roses with leafless stems
We disappear into the shadows surrounding

Sometimes we live in someone's mind
A stolen heart beating
Like the ageless sages left their bodies naked
Their minds trapped in the Himalayan mist
We see the dreams belong to someone
Unleashing it on a kite
Trusting the line we never control
Blotted ink stain covering the obituary column
Hiding everything under

Hero & Heroine

WHEN THE CUCKOO broke the long silence to coo eight times, Nila was already awake. She ignored it and continued to flirt with the sunlight intruding into her bedroom through the slits of the red velvet window drapes. As she tilted her golden anklets, she reflected the light to make tiny stardust around Lord Krishna's picture hung on the wall. The clock was her companion in seclusion, and a major reason for the little tension that fumed between them in the initial days she moved to the US. The sound of the cuckoo gave her a false feeling that she was close to her home, and all her dear ones were within walking distance away.

"No human can survive you, Chatterbox, not even this mechanical bird." That was how Ashok made fun of her when she argued to have the cuckoo clock go off every fifteen minutes, like the Grandfather clock in her parent's home. Ashok reasoned this bizarre behavior to be part of Nila's loneliness, and the creative mind she claimed to have. He always hesitated to satisfy Nila's demands as he could never understand her reasoning, but later he always succumbed to avoid ruining the serenity.

For Nila, when her husband was at work, the clock gave her comfort and curbed her loneliness. It was a companion who patiently listened to her crazy thoughts and nodded at regular intervals. Cuckoo was the most ideal friend she could ever ask for, as it had all the qualities to get along with an extrovert like her. It had the patience to listen to all her whims and all her never-ending stories. The cuckoo clock was a wedding gift from Auntie Molly, someone who was very dear to her, the one who took care of her and was there for her as her own mother from the day she was born.

When Ashok's marriage proposal came for their arranged marriage, everyone in the family thought he was the perfect match for Nila. He was well-educated and exceptionally well mannered, but there was a fear in everyone to send her off in marriage to a faraway place like America, with very different customs. It was Auntie Molly who convinced everyone and stood as the guarantor for the wedding. Auntie and her husband Alex lived in a place close to Ashok's city, which gave everyone confidence. In case something needed to be looked into, Auntie was only a few hours away.

It was a long-awaited day for Nila… a trip to Auntie's home. This was something she had wanted to do in the first month of her arrival in the US, but it had taken almost a year to happen. It had been postponed a few times with Ashok's work commitments. This time she had left everything to God, and prayed fervently to Lord Ganesh, the ultimate power, to confiscate any obstacles, to avoid any last-minute delays in their travel plans. She had picked the dress to wear the day before and baked a fruitcake a few days earlier. She planned a surprise for Auntie by making a collage with pictures from her collection she began gathering from her primary school days and onward.

"Wake up, Ashok, let's get ready quickly, and start at nine as we planned last night." Nila shook her husband to wake him.

"Come on, you are not even letting me sleep late on a long weekend? There is nothing much to get ready. A quick shower and I will be on the road. It's you who needs two hours to put makeup on and delays everything," he continued in a mocking voice. "You know the later we go the less we need to listen to the so-called Uncle Alex's fake stories of bravery. Even a cook retired from the military would claim to have shot down a helicopter." He chuckled.

"Shut up, Ashok; you should respect people who risked their lives for their country. He is a gentleman. And you know what? He is a very successful businessman owning several gas stations in the city. I hope he is home and not busy when we get there."

"I bet he will be there, especially when he has admirers like you wanting to listen to him." Ashok sounded like a whining kid, jealous over losing importance in the eyes of his wife.

Nila continued in a broken voice, "Ashok; you don't know how dear they are to me. You will realize how nice they are one day; they are probably far better than anyone you have ever met."

"Oh… let us not go further on that," Ashok replied, confining her. Nila jumped out of the bed to show her frustration and went to the living room, where she always found something to calm herself down with.

She looked through the pictures on the collage she had made as a gift for Auntie. She began to cheer a little while looking at a faded picture that was taken with a Polaroid camera. The picture was sent to her after Auntie Molly had reached the US for the first time. She looked thin and pale, but beautiful, with the statue of Liberty in the backdrop. Auntie had written behind the picture that she had to be in New York for a month, to attend training before she could begin to work. Glancing through the pictures from her childhood made Nila nostalgic and brought memories to dampen her eyes.

ALTHOUGH AUNTIE MOLLY was not her mother's younger sister or even related to her in any way, Nila used to call her *Chitta*. But all the kids in the neighborhood began to address her as 'Auntie' after she came to the village to visit for the first time since leaving for the US. They felt that treating her like a local woman may not be appropriate, and they found delight in calling her "American Auntie." A big crowd of relatives and neighbors had gathered in their home to celebrate her arrival. Kids were playing in the backyard and around the haystack waiting for Auntie to arrive from the airport, which was a three-hour car journey. When the wind bustled, or the water wheel in the rice field swayed with a sudden gush, kids ran into the dirt road screaming, "She is here!" and waited until the sound faded away. They all waited, hoping to eat a stomach full of chocolates and candies when she opened her luggage. After a long wait, when *Chitta* got out of the black ambassador car, almost everyone wowed and had their eyebrows arched in astonishment.

The change from a naïve village girl into a sophisticated *American Madam* was not something the poor villagers could digest easily. Everyone looked in disbelief at the one who had left clad in a saree to return in jeans and top. Her long hair was cut by half and curled at the tip. With her threaded eyebrows and glossy lips, she looked like a celebrity on the cover page of *Vanitha* Malayalam women's magazine. Kids hesitated to go near her until a naughty kid screamed, "Our *American-Madaamma* is finally here." Everyone laughed in amusement. Nila didn't go near her at first because she felt a distance she'd never had before. But the kids who went near her said she had a beautiful smell that was sweeter than the Arabian perfume worn by people returning from Dubai.

In those days, Auntie was the topic of conversation in the local tea stalls and corner shops where people gathered to gossip and smoke locally made *beedi*. Some pranksters even spread the rumor that she was there to look for a new husband after she got tired of her American husband.

Auntie Molly's family had been their neighbor way before Nila was born. But, they were more than just neighbors; they were part of the family, always around, tending to and spending time in their home. Molly was the oldest and sweetest amongst the four girls. Amma once told her how they came to the village. They were part of a group of *Syrian Christian* families who migrated from Kottayam in the Travancore region. Those hardworking families turned the barren, rocky land, inhabited by poisonous snakes, into plantations. Her father, Mathaichan, was a sincere and honest man. When communism was spreading in the area, he helped Nila's father settle the labor dispute and protect the family from an ambush common against landlords at that time. People in the village respected him, and due to the booming tourism industry, they even named the northern hill in his name as Mathai Mala. It's now been renamed to Mathew Hills. Mathaichan toiled to turn that rocky hill into green, filling it with tapioca plants, a remnant from the Portuguese invasion a few centuries ago. *Kappa* produced from the plants later became the staple food for the poor in the whole region. Later, he was the one who introduced rubber trees to the region, which made most peasants rich.

Mathaichan used to work from early morning till the sundown, cultivating yucca known as *Kappa* locally, and rubber trees on the hill, and rice in the rice field. On Friday evenings, he walked to the other side of the hill to drink *Arrack,* homemade liquor made by distilling toddy from the coconut palm. On his way home, he bought sizzling *Parippu-vada,* lentil discs fried in coconut oil, from the teashop. All the kids waited for the treat. Drunk and zigzagging back home, he made sure the *Parippu-vada* was still fresh. He kept them warm covered in layers of newspaper under his armpit. He turned his armpit into a walking oven!

They all sat on the half wall of portico eating Parippu-vada, then got a stomach full of skinned *kappa,* boiled and cooked along with fresh hot pepper sauce. Nila's mom fried sardines dipped in spicy sauce to go along with the *Kappa.* Once tired of eating, they all went down to the courtyard and sat around a kerosene lamp. Then Mathaichan would sing folk songs from Kottayam, and teach them *Margam Kali,* a traditional dance played to songs narrating the stories based on the evangelization by St. Thomas, the Apostle, in India.

Friday nights gave everyone vivid memories that none of them would ever forget. But like an untimely monsoon that blazed through the sky and drowned everything below, strings of trage-dies charred all their dreams in its fury.

On a sunny, humid morning, while Mathaichan was clearing the weeds among tapioca plant bushes, a saw-scaled viper blended among the dry leaves pressed its fangs into his left lower calf, filling it with venom. He quickly turned around and chopped the snake into two halves before he collapsed. It was only after an hour that his wife, Susanna, found him while bringing him breakfast. He was unconscious with froth all over his mouth. She screamed for help, and he was taken to the village *vishahari,* the local poison specialist, but he couldn't do much. His foot had turned black by then and later at the government hospital, doctors amputated the dead foot from below his knee. The venom that took the foot of the breadwinner also cast a dark shadow over the life of four girls and their helpless mother. As a healthy man, he never sat idle or fell sick in his entire life. He was struggling to handle his new situation. Later, his courage and physical strength drained. It didn't get any better. Following monsoon hit his fields sending a gushing mudslide that took out all the hard work he had put in for decades. That was too much for him to handle. His health deteriorated quickly, his frail mind and ailing body couldn't survive that rainy season.

Nila's family was there for his family, but it was hard to go through. When Molly decided to go to America, the family finally emerged from the years-long haze and pain. Their story was a living lesson for Nila and everyone who knew them. Nila always found strength, as it didn't matter how weak one was or the graveness of troubles one went through, what really mattered was finding a way to keep the mind strong and fearlessly fighting the fight to overcome one's own fears. The family struggled to survive. To make their living, Molly quit going to school and helped her mom doing menial chores for many affluent families. After a few years of struggle, and seeing no way to bounce back to normalcy, Molly joined a convent to become a nun. There she completed high school and studied nursing to serve the poor in the remote villages of northern India. During that time, Nila was a school girl and Auntie used to visit her home once every year. She always stopped at Nila's home to see her first, as there was an inherent bond between them. She was there always when Nila grew up, and she was like her own child. Amma used to tell Nila that when she was little she used to cry hysterically for hours until Auntie held her.

On every visit, Auntie gifted Nila with oversized woolen sweaters donated to the monastery by people living in western countries. After she completed her studies, a missionary priest who knew about her family's dismal state asked Auntie to leave the order to help her family and arranged for her to go to America.

Nila recalled the day Auntie left for America. Everyone followed the slow-moving white ambassador car, biding Molly goodbye along the way, until it reached the train station. Keeping all her emotions to herself, Molly smiled and waved while standing at the train door. Everyone watched her as the train disappeared over those parallel lines that merged in the distance. They all wept, as they all loved her and knew they may not see her for a very long time. But the mood transformed into a happy one when they all turned to see her mother smiling, which hardly anyone had seen in a long time. She had learned that tears were worth more when shed in joy.

Nila wiped her teary eyes with the back of her hand, and continued staring at the old pictures in the living room.

～ゝ

It was past noon by the time they reached Auntie Molly's home. Stepping out of the car into the driveway, they got a taste of the warmth that was waiting for them. The over-worked kitchen exhaust fan continued to swirl the smell of freshly fried beef cutlets and curried fish into the entire neighborhood. Unable to hold their excitement, Auntie and Uncle came running outside to receive them. Stroking Nila's arm, Auntie said with affection, "We were worried… Did you get lost on the way?"

"Oh, no, we started a little late. There was construction on the way," Nila said with an ecstatic smile.

Except for the thick mustache with tips pointed up like the old Air India mascot, Uncle looked nothing like a typical retired Indian military person. He had long curly hair which hung loosely just above the shoulders, hanging out of his baseball cap. The cap was there to cover his shiny bald head that was evident by the smooth forehead and thin sideburns His small round pot-belly complemented his happy face and puffy cheeks. Shallow eyes showed he was as sincere as he looked. The smile on his face and the attention he gave them spilled over with love and affection in his heart. Ashok instantly fell for Uncle's simplicity, and his reluctance at coming disappeared instantly.

"Come, children, come. Let's go in." Uncle in his affectionate voice persuaded them.

"Wow!" Nila was amazed by the gorgeous home and scanned

the inside while removing her sandals. The Cathedral Ceiling with a gigantic French chandelier and the large bay windows in the living room, gave the home a Grande look. After sitting on the hand-carved Chinese sofa, Ashok peaked out of the window that overlooked a large pond with a private walking trail around it. Two snow-white swans were idly floating by. As they looked at each other, they made a squished heart symbol with their long necks.

From the kitchen, Nila walked toward the family room, browsing the Italian themed-cabinets built around the fireplace in dark cherry wood. Its contents displayed a snapshot of their artistic taste. Ashok joined Nila looking at the miniature house-boats with elephants carved in the teak wood. Chess pieces in crystal were arranged without the board. The pawns had been chiseled to look like human faces which Ashok thought had probably been picked by their children. A shelf at the top was filled with trophies and medals their kids had won during their school days. Above the TV were spotlights that sparkled on their magnificent stone collection. Some of them had silver and gold sparkling.

Auntie opened the glass door and took out a small shiny stone. She pointed at the golden flecks stuck on it and said, "This is real gold, see? All the jewelry we have used to be like this. We got this from South Dakota when we visited Mount Rushmore, where the presidents' faces are carved on a mountain."

Nila felt the stone and excitedly said, "Auntie, we should buy stones like this instead of too much gold jewelry. Jewelry stays in the box most of the time, but people get to enjoy it if it is something sizable and displayed like this." Everyone agreed and cheered, appreciating Nila's intended humor.

Left of the cabinet was busy with framed photographs of family members organized in different phases of their lives. The golden family tree fascinated Ashok and Nila as it held pictures of different eras and fashions. Ashok looked once again at the leaf that had Uncle's picture in; he had no mustache and looked to be in his twenties.

"Your daughter looks exactly like you twenty years ago." Nila noticed the close resemblance of Auntie from her old picture collections.

Auntie responded with a smile. "She is in pre-med at Stanford University. Our son is doing his final year of Civil Engineering at Villanova University."

Nila nodded her head in appreciation and commented, "He is so handsome. Girls must be going crazy!"

Everyone exploded in laughter and Uncle added, "They'll both be here in the last week of August. You should definitely come over to meet them then."

While everyone chatted, Auntie had covered the large kitchen table with snacks that she had prepared. Everything was as Nila remembered from her childhood. Seeing a plateful of golden *Parippu-vada,* she was taken back to those old days, remembering Auntie's dad whose picture was in a place of pride on the family wall.

"Molly, please bring some snacks downstairs, let me show Ashok the basement," Uncle said.

"Don't spoil the kid, he is not like you," Auntie said in a scolding but jovial voice and continued, "Nila, don't worry. Unless he shows his *Kottayam* style of hospitality, there won't be peace in this home until the next time you come."

Uncle smiled and gave his wife a friendly wink, "Come, Ashok, let's go downstairs." He got up from the couch and walked to the basement and Ashok followed him. Nila felt awful. She feared if Ashok were left alone with her so called bragging uncle, she would end up paying a big price when they got back home. But she was relieved later when she heard from Ashok what had truly happened in the basement while she chatted with Auntie.

~

THE BASEMENT LOOKED even more fabulous than the main area of the home. Its walls had original art pieces and paintings depicting the beauty of South India. A life-sized replica of a golden caparison, which is used to cover an elephant's trunk for temple festivals, was displayed on the wall. It welcomed everyone to the basement with a Kerala pride. Next to it was a large brightly colored mask depicting the expression of a *Kathakali* dancer. A world-famous handmade *Aranmula* mirror, a metallurgical wonder from Kerala, made Ashok feel like he was in an art museum. He felt the super smooth furniture with his fingers and had a quick peek at the beautiful home theater adjacent to the main hall. Ashok was amazed and he felt privileged to be in a country that had the magic of giving a retired military man from a humble beginning, and having barely finished high school, the opportunity to live such an enviable lifestyle.

Uncle turned the lights on in the other end of the basement and chortled to himself. "Come, let us sit and relax in my favorite spot in this world."

Ashok was stunned when the corner of the basement was lit up. He was overwhelmed as he approached a bar that looked more magnificent than the one in a high-end restaurant. *It would surely prompt a non-drinker to consume alcohol*, Ashok thought. He gazed at the rare collection of bottles of all shapes that had come from all around the world and was amused by a bottle with a fruit way larger than the bottle's neck. There was also a bottle, which came with gold dust in it, and a few others had dead worms in them he thought was disgusting.

"All these bottles are waiting to be tasted, which one do you want to start with?" Uncle joked to encourage him to feel free.

"I am not big into drinking, Uncle. Sometimes, I have a couple of beers with friends."

"Oh, my son, don't disappoint me." Uncle continued to chuckle.

Ashok responded, "Of course, I will give you company and go with whatever you suggest."

Uncle was happy with this response. It was clear from his excitement that Uncle was looking forward to having a few drinks with Ashok. He pulled a bottle from the cabinet and began to tell Ashok about his tastes and passions when it comes to drinking habits. Uncle Alex drank only Old Monk Rum, which he claimed to be his 'Regular Use Medicine' that stood for RUM, a habit he picked up while serving the Indian military guarding the border with Pakistan. He picked up a taste for it to survive the brutal Himalayan cold, and to elude the boredom that could have eroded his sharpness.

He believed he had something in common with the Old Monk Rum; they were both first brewed in the sacred Himalayan Mountains with the souls of sages guarding over them. Those souls traveled hundreds of miles, away from their physical bodies that were still alive in the caverns hidden under the snow-covered mountains. He always felt their presence when he sipped each drop of it. His friend, who was a liquor store owner, ordered and shipped it to him from India when he ran out. Ashok watched Uncle pour the drink over the ice cubes into the crystal glasses.

Uncle raised his glass toward Ashok. "Cheers! This is not just a drink, it is a medicine. It heals the heart if you ever had a broken one, it puts your mind straight, and it will let you fight till you win." He laughed and took a long sip.

Sitting at an awkward angle, pushing on the footrest on the

counter, Ashok tried to sit looking straight, and he almost lost balance and swiveled toward the left wall. His heart stopped for a moment, as he faced a wild animal. A large, stuffed buck head was hiding behind the Budweiser beer neon light on the wall. Its face was tilted down with shiny eyes looking toward him. For a moment, he thought it still had life in its eyes. Below the antlers, there was large framed picture of beautiful Dal Lake in the midst of Himalayan Mountains. Pointed lights made the snowcap and the houseboat roofs glow giving an extra charm to the place.

Ashok was surprised to see a real trophy buck and was curious to know how it ended up on their basement wall. Uncle told him he used to spend days in the woods on stands amid thick cover, waiting. Though he was trained to kill intruders on the border, he never had to take anyone's life but had many antlers. Auntie didn't know about his hobby for a long time. Even though she worked as a surgery nurse, she was still scared of blood and didn't like him doing it. She even threatened him saying she would run away. Uncle was not joking; Auntie had no guilt around eating steak or fried fish but couldn't digest the idea of him hunting.

Taking a quick sip out of the glass, Uncle said with pride, "It is a fourteen pointer and my last one."

Ashok couldn't resist suppressing his curiosity. He asked why he quit hunting as he thought Auntie might have discovered his secret endeavors at some point, and might have threatened to leave him.

Uncle tried to avoid answering, then he gazed at the trophy for a moment and said, "She never found out, but you know we are all brave when we are young. We dare to do anything and never think of the consequences. The moment you know you are going to become a father, you are no longer the same person… your blood no longer flows as fast as your thoughts run." Ashok sensed Uncle was not very comfortable as his voice cracked, but he didn't hinder and he continued his story.

"I watched the buck enter the cut cornfield, and I knew the stage was set; it was a three hundred pounder. The shot was taken at sixty yards and it went a bit too high. The buck went down like a rock, but soon it was on its feet and charged back into the woods. By the time I came down from the cover, it was not anywhere to be seen. There were several hoof marks where it had thrashed around before gaining its feet. I followed the blood trail marks and in ten minutes I saw him; he had fallen dead in the middle of the field. When I walked toward him, I saw a female deer next to him. Her belly was fully bulged and veins netted it. I could see her tummy shaking with its fawn kicking. She stared into my eyes; I couldn't look at her again. I don't know how the deer family works, but at that moment I thought of my wife who was pregnant at the time. After that day, I couldn't hunt anymore."

By the time he finished the story, glasses were empty and Uncle refilled them quickly. Ashok was guilty for exposing the softer side of a brave soldier. He badly wanted to lighten the mood so he looked toward the beautiful scenery of Kashmir below the Antilles and began to appreciate its details.

"This ambience of Lake Dal looks so mesmerizing with the backdrop of the snow-covered Himalayas."

Noticing Ashok's keenness in the picture, Uncle asked "Don't you love this picture? Have you ever been to Kashmir?"

Ashok shook his head.

"Oh dear, you are missing a lot… if there is heaven on Earth, that's the place." Uncle showed his passion for the Kashmir and continued, "You should rent a *Shikara,* the traditional boat in the Dal Lake. Have a couple of drinks, and just stare into the Himalayas. When the sun sets, watch the sky changing colors like the passion of a Kashmiri folk dancer dancing in the moonlight till daybreak. The silver light will fade away to pour diamonds over the sky, filling it with stars you have never seen in such abundance.

The oar and the waves will beat with the rhythm of your heart. The cool breeze will caress you, bringing the mystic music held in the heart of those mountains that you haven't heard. Soon you will be in a place you have never been; your mind will be one with the soul of the Himalayas and it will make you feel like you were there forever, and none of your worries had ever existed. Trust me; you will never want to leave."

He paused and turned into a philosopher. "There is something about Himalayan air. You know monks and sadhus don't feel cold. They don't feed their body; they don't age but live beyond centuries. Unlike them, we worry about the past and are anxious about the future, forgetting to live in the present. We search for peace in the midst of chaos. Like a giant bubble we try to fill ourselves with our own ego only to see it burst into nothing, forgetting how tiny we are in this universe. Dust ... but we ..." Stifling back his feeling Uncle didn't bother to complete where he was going with his thoughts.

"Uncle, now I believe in this drink, it certainly has some magical powers. It has not only made a brave Indian soldier and a businessman out of you, but a philosopher and an amazing poet, too." Ashok couldn't stop expressing his admiration. In his mind he thought Uncle's life could be a plot for an Indian movie, except he had to handle all the archetypes and characters as he was in unison with all the archetypes, like the Tamil Movie *Dasaavatharam*, where the actor Kamal Hasan portrayed ten characters simultaneously.

"Next time you visit your parents, you both should definitely make a trip to Kashmir." Uncle tried to persuade him.

"I'd love to go there but... it is always in the news for bad reasons, terrorism and unrest. We will... when things settle."

Uncle, with an uproarious laugh, raised his glass in one hand. Then with the other, he twirled the tip of his mustache between his thumb and forefinger. Clearing his throat, he said, "What you have heard of Militants is from the media, right?"

Ashok nodded in agreement.

"I have seen them, I have walked with them, and I have fought with them," Uncle disclosed.

"Wow. That takes a lot of courage," Ashok said.

Uncle continued, "Well, we all live with some kind of fear, but the moments when we have to conquer our fears, our hearts pump faster to make our nerves stronger than steel. Our senses fall into safety mode, our lungs turn quieter and our heart beats in silence. Haven't you noticed your system wouldn't let you sneeze when you were in hiding and afraid of being found?"

Ashok replied, "I agree. Being part of the military must have helped you handle a lot of situations better."

"Of course it did. Anyone who got posted along the 285 kilometers on the line of control in the Jammu-Pakistan border would have a different view of life if they were lucky enough to come home alive."

Noticing Ashok's keenness to listen to his story, and being in a good mood, Uncle began to share his daring tales. He was posted at a picket, along a hostile terrain, to guard a highly dangerous and remote location in Kashmir on the India-Pakistan border. They were a team of two, taking turns patrolling and watching vigilantly from the observation tower. Their home base was several miles away, reachable only by air in winter. It was decades ago; primitive Russian surveillance equipment could never cut through. There were no unbreakable fences like today. The border was just an imaginary line, and two angry barracks stood facing each other on either side.

Below the flag poles through the gaps in the barrack walls, each side had artilleries placed that pointed toward each other. Heaps of grenades, semi-automatic weapons, and magazines took a giant portion of the living space in the barracks, leaving just enough room to crawl into the sleeping bag. Gunshots and shells flew over them each night like a ritual. When the real alert came from the base, they were ready in a few seconds. The real enemy was not the one everyone thought. Infiltrating terrorists from the training camps on the other side was ongoing in the cover of the darkness, making the region unstable. They were always prepared when they arrived, but the infiltrators took more risk in the wind that came with a bone-rattling chill and almost zero visibility. Most times Mother Nature failed them and the following day they would see many frozen bodies over the terrain.

The saying, 'keep your friends close, and your enemies closer' literally made sense in their case. Two enemy pickets waited and watched each other's moves constantly, building tension with every moment. During the day, they didn't even know if they should smile at each other and they exchanged unfriendly stares with the opposite side, continuing to do their surveillance and chores by taking turns. Intermittent songs caught by the transistor radio kept them entertained, something they look forward to in the late afternoons.

How long can you look at someone angrily for? The mind is like the sky; sometimes it clears and brightens. Their attitude was changed by a little idea that sprung between them. It was on a *Diwali*, a festival that symbolized the victory of good over evil. The food delivery crew dropped them an extra-large box of sweets. Alok, his partner, suggested giving this to the barracks on the other side, their enemy. He pointed out that Pakistani soldiers supported them with fires when an infiltration of terrorists occurred. Terrorists were their common enemy. They both agreed on the idea of sharing the joy of *Diwali* with the other side, but the big question was how to deliver the box? The moment one crosses the border, the enemy fire could swallow him. Even in death, disgrace would follow for crossing the international border without following the proper procedures. After deliberate discussion, they decided to throw the packet to the other side. Then to gain attention, they fired into the sky, the same way the other side celebrated their holidays. They watched through the slits in the wall of the barracks. Three of them quickly went out with guns pointing and stood in position ready to attack. Uncle went out, gathering all his courage with his hands in the air, and wished them "Happy Diwali" and pointed toward the box of sweets.

From that day onwards nothing changed how they operated, but they were friends, friendship without borders. They used to share food, play cards. The relief of not having to fear something that burdened the mind forever is indeed the greatest gift of one's freedom. As time passed, and the minds got lighter with less worries, they stayed focused on the common enemy. When there were tensions between the two countries, or one was getting the message from the base of danger, they used to shoot at the other bunker's direction without hurting anyone. On some nights when it was really quiet, they used to gather to play cards and sip from their rationed Old Monk Rum.

It was during one of those rivalries that Alex expressed his wild dream of going down the mountain to explore the countryside of Pakistan-owned Kashmir. He craved to get stoned drinking *bhang*, which was a very popular drink made from cannabis in that region. Everyone laughed and thought he was crazy. Indeed, it was a crazy idea as it was unthinkable. It was true that when the brain has nothing to keep it busy, the blood will hesitate to flow and slows down to diminish the brain cells. It was obvious that the consequences of getting caught were beyond what anyone could think, but it didn't matter to him. He was certain it wouldn't be limited to undergoing court-martial, losing jobs, or getting jailed. In addition, it would invite huge disgrace to the family, the 'betrayer' tab would follow for generations. But nothing worried him with rum in his belly; he was young and was mad about going to the enemy's den to get high.

After a few days, one of the Pak soldiers, Fayyaz, offered to take Uncle along with him when they went to collect rations and supplies. On the way, there was a place hidden in the mountains where he could have his wishes fulfilled, then come back when they returned. He joined the Pak soldier, disguising himself as a native traveler, carrying enough local money and his military outfit in the backpack.

Hiking down the steep mountainous area was so grueling; it took more than courage and skill. A slip or a wrong step on the narrow path could make one vanish into the steep ravines, where even the bones would disappear into dust. Journey in winter was impossible and a helicopter dropped supplies every other week. The risk was worth it for the lifetime experience of seeing the breathtaking view of the gorges and multi-layered glaciers on the faraway mountains. The shiny strip of river looked like a silver necklace thrown onto the green. After an hour, they reached a place hidden from the world. It had a few wooden and stone houses that were stacked together like a honeycomb. The stone houses on the edge looked as if they were carved on the mountain with tiny passages between them. His friend, the Pakistani soldier, walked into a stone house with a wide wooden door.

Uncle had no idea what was waiting for him inside. As he entered, a seething air swept over him. Its pungent stench opened up every pore in his body, and his blood seemed to inhale it so much that he lost all his sensations. He feared suffocation for a moment and felt his nostrils to make sure he was still breathing. Slowly his blurry eyes cleared, and he began to see shadows moving among the smoke from the hundreds of hookahs lit like a thousand fireflies stuck to it.

With a soothing grin, Fayyaz said. "Don't worry, you will get used to it. It is a once in a lifetime experience. Have no worries.

No fears. I will go down and get supplies, and grab you on my way back. Enjoy!"

He disappeared into the backroom for a while and went on his way. After few minutes of waiting, a boy around ten-years-old came with a clay pot filled with a dull green drink. He took a sip and another sip and another and soon it was all gone. Another full pot replaced the empty one. He noticed voices dragging but smiles brightened every face. For him, it was like watching a slow-moving movie where he sat idle in a corner of the screen, unnoticed. He snapped in and out of reality and slowly blended into the air and the smell bothered him no more.

First, he thought he was hallucinating. His hazy eyes zoomed in on a woman in a burka approaching him. She sat opposite to him and asked, "Sir, would you like to smoke with some herbs, your friend told me to take care of you as well." She keenly watched him drink from the pot through the netted cover on her face.

"So, I guess you are not from here, right? No one drinks this way here."

For a moment, she lifted the cover over her face, giggled and whispered, "Relax, India boy," and quickly walked away. He was stirred and ecstatic at the same time. His eyes followed her till she merged into clouds of smoke that whirled around on her path.

Did she reveal my identity aloud? Or was that just a fluke? Either way, she couldn't be harmful, he thought. Unsure he was, but her enigmatic face and ardent eyes made him curious and sparked an incomprehensible feeling within. He began to inhale the dazed vapor into his heart. Craning, he looked through the smoke circles he exhaled, hoping to see her again. Suddenly, it occurred to him that she didn't belong there, and he had the strong urge to know more about her. For a man in his early twenties, it was his instincts and the feeling that made him keep going; experiences and veracities were hindrances.

It was not just for a good time, but the urge to see her was driving Uncle Alex to keep visiting the joint. Some days she ignored him for no obvious reason, other days she would cling to him. Later that year, at the beginning of *Ramadan* season, he went down the mountain. The door was closed and he knocked and waited patiently. There was no sign of anyone inside and he turned to go back, but his heart didn't. He knocked really hard, and then stuck his ear to the tiny slit on the wooden door. He listened for any movements inside. After few minutes of waiting, he heard a feeble sound of footsteps approaching; he quickly recognized the movement.

She opened the door slowly to have a peek at the visitor who was at the door. When she saw him, she lifted the cover over her face and let him in. The place was empty, but he could hear people walking and murmurs were coming from inside the kitchen area.

"Do you know this place is closed this month till the sun sets?"

He shook his head while he seated himself on a worn-out divan. After fetching a pot of cold bhang, she sat opposite him and lit a hookah for him. She stared at him, her blazing eyes pierced into his and he felt a burn somewhere inside his chest. He was a bit embarrassed by the situation, but as a soldier trained to fight against the toughest enemies in the brutal situations, he was able to gain his composure quickly and asked, "Is it real or the stench of the stale air from the past that is driving me crazy?"

"Do you come here because you like this place? Or anyway… you are not in love. Are you?" she asked him in a soft voice.

Stammering, he replied, "No… no, of course not. I haven't thought of such a thing." Saying that, he quickly gulped what was left in the pot. She took the empty pot inside to get him another one. To overcome the uneasiness of the past episode, he took a few quick puffs from the hookah, rekindling the dying ember.

While bringing the refilled pot, she asked him, "Do you know who I am? You know nothing about the lives under this roof. This burqa is just a smooth cover; you really don't want to breathe what is burning inside."

There was silence for few minutes. They avoided looking at each other, and then after a long pause she began to tell her story.

Her name was Shalini, a Hindu girl from Kashmir. She was abducted one afternoon when she was walking home after school. She was taken to their hideout in the nearby forest where she was brutally tortured and beaten for several days. They hit her with a rod on her thighs, threatened to kill her family if she did not change her religion and marry one of the militant leaders. Uncle had sat speechless in disbelief. He was taking tiny sips from the pot to control his mounting angst.

"I am not the only one; it always happens to young women and teenage girls in Jammu and Kashmir. Many dreams are shattered at gunpoint, forcing us to save ourselves without any choice." There was a fire in her eyes when she said this.

She wanted to study and become a teacher, but her dreams were shattered after she was forcibly married to a militant. Ten months after her marriage, her childhood was snatched away when she delivered a son, but he died before he turned one.

"I didn't cry," she continued to speak from her heart. "You see those children working here... he would have been one of them, eventually forced to cross the border to carry out a ruthless mission. Maybe God loved him more than anyone else. He saved him before he blew himself up along with innocent people." She rubbed away her tears, but they kept dripping through her fingers. Uncle had closed his eyes for a moment to see a school girl with kohl-lined eyes walking through the stone paved road;

her eventful life and her fate had brought her before him. *Why am I here listening to her? How can I give her hope?* He pondered.

Failure to find a way to console her made him feel tiny. Resentment brewed within him for his own helplessness. It turned into a feeling he couldn't control. He left in silence, hoping to come back, to give her reasons to be buoyant; he didn't promise anything as he didn't want her to fail again. His feelings toward her deepened and its warmth shielded him from the stinging cold air wanting to pierce through his spirit.

Uncle visited her whenever the weather was favorable and tension along the border was trivial. During winter afternoons, she snuck out with him to the valley as a couple might and hung out in Sufi shrines. They hid in its crowded basement where the rising intensity of *Qawwali* music made them disappear into a trance, wrapping them in the intoxicating fumes that pervaded its ambience. Some days they exited the present, dancing with the spirits of the saints who took them to a rapturous state. Those were the best days of their lives which they hoped would last forever, but the aura of the saints' fire enveloping them didn't help to outlive their fate.

It was at the end of one of their outings when everything changed for good. When they returned it was night, the whole valley was under curfew. Like an unending thunder rolling, flairs and sounds from shelling and gunfire emerged all along the border. Helicopters were searching with floodlights, which lit every nook and corner of the region's darkness. It was rumored that hundreds of trained militants had infiltrated into the Indian Territory. His entire body trembled, resonating with his drumming heartbeat, and he struggled hard to regain his composure. Neither the chilling northwest wind nor the relaxation techniques learned in the military academy could keep him cool. His precarious situation, brought on by himself, and the thought of the consequences of his inane actions, made him nervous. He weighed the graveness of living in the brutal Pakistani jail from where he might never see the sunshine for the rest of his life. And if he was spotted by the Indian helicopter in the Pakistan territory, he would be stamped as a betrayer for life, to live in disgrace.

Shalini came close to him. After wiping the sweat off his forehead, she slowly ran her fingers through his ruffled hair and said, "Hey, brave soldier, you are born to fight fearlessly, and to face even death with a smile. The storm will be over; you know what could be the worst thing that could happen to you. You could join me here; a long burqa will protect you when you are here." He stood up, looked at her, and slowly lifted her face cover and looked into her eyes. He whispered in her ear, "Don't you know, in this burqa I will look much more beautiful than you?" They both burst into laughter and all his worries disappeared, at least for the moment.

He waited a few hours for everything to calm down, and for the border to come to some kind of normalcy. Then he cut through the bushes and fog to the place where his uniform and gun were hidden. He changed into the military outfit and hiked toward the border that was almost a mile away from the picket. The nourishing cold wind gave him the strength to be himself and he felt he had already won the greatest war and was ready to take on another one.

When he reached the border, he looked up at the dull, gray sky and took a deep breath. Then he closed his eyes and jumped into the trench that was dug very deep to keep the enemies from crossing. Everything else was just a distant memory from there. When he opened the eyes, he was in the military hospital, covered in a body cast. He had several broken bones and had a severe back injury. It took almost six months for his treatment and rehabilitation before he went back to duty.

Uncle then pointed toward a medal that was hung on the wall and said, "Can you believe it? That was the Medal of Honor I received for that night. My colleague covered me. He said I volunteered to go check out some suspicious movement on the border and didn't see me after that. Even the helicopters couldn't find me until the next morning. My pictures were in the newspaper."

Ashok couldn't wait to hear the closure of the story and asked, "Did you meet her again?"

Dissolving into silent laughter, Uncle replied, "After recovering, they felt I wouldn't be fit enough for combat jobs. I was posted in New Delhi at a desk job. I really wanted to go back and cross the border to see her again. But our wishes rarely align with fate. See… now I am here on the other side of the world sipping Old Monk with you, recreating my memories to live in."

Ashok didn't know what to say, but he recited verses from the Indian epic Mahabharata where Lord Krishna advised the confused *Pandava* prince *Arjuna* over the battle of *Kurukshetra*.

"Whatever happened, happened for the good;
Whatever is happening, is happening for the good;
Whatever will happen, will also happen for the good only.
You need not have any regrets for the past.
You need not worry for the future.
The present is happening …"

BY THE TIME Ashok and Nila headed home, it was dark and they didn't speak to each other. Nila was worried. Ashok would scold her for leaving him alone to the garrulous uncle to die of boredom. But Ashok was in the hangover period of the most breathtaking stories he had heard from an uncle, which Nila had no clue about. During this trip, Ashok realized his outlook on life and people had changed quite a bit. Uncle Alex, a simple man whom he believed to be just a loquacious bragger, helped him redefine his views. He always felt that he had nothing to contribute and he took ordinary lives for granted. He realized everyone was different with unique experiences and had a role to play in this big world. While on the highway, they had old, nostalgic Hindi songs playing in the background. While passing through a *deer crossing* warning sign, Ashok remembered Uncle's hunting story. He would slow down for every road-kill on the way to see if there was someone in tears waiting nearby.

Maya's departure.
Gone to airport.
It rained so hard... really a
sad day

Life is a river
Bearing the burden and color from where it began;
Meandering through sandy banks, thick forests,
Seizing the scent and trapping its beats.

Pebbles—nestled dreams carried along,
Abandoned on the way to delay its destiny.
Lonely traveler in the midst of chaos
A wrecked heart through the torrents

Knowledge rains into wisdom
Like the hills and valley gathering water
Filling the veined streams to nourish
The creases and grooves that hold the brain's secrets
But mountains fold and their ridges hide their stories
We look at beaten deadwood floating
Searching for the reasons
We strip the dry moss on ravines for traces

Under the slanting tree, standing
Like a discontented fisherman
Stretching a broken rod into the river
We hope to hold its rage and despair,
We sit staring into the vacant memory
Breathing the air that kisses its waters
Listening to the song it never stops humming

Life in a Faceless World

POLICE OFFICERS ON Segways were swiftly making their routine patrol, scanning everyone on their way. As usual, the TSA officers were scanning passports and faces for some resemblances, without spilling even a hint of a grin at the anxious passengers.

After passing through the security check, Maya paused for a moment, then slowly turned towards Nila and her husband Ashok to say her final goodbye. She was trying to bring out her best smile, hiding the tears in her puffy eyes. She failed miserably upon seeing her friend, Nila, break down in tears. Ashok averted his eyes and stared at the baby perched on Maya's hip, and bid goodbye. Ashok gently rubbed Nila's back to console her. By the time they came out of the departure area, the rain had just stopped, and the naked sky had nothing but more vacuum to fill inept hopes. The street between the airport building and the parking lot had almost flooded due to the storm that had just passed, and traffic was at a standstill. Ashok and Nila, blanketed in a harrowing silence, walked through the skyway to the parking lot.

Maybe Nila wants to cocoon herself or dissolve into a world of solitude, Ashok thought. She sank into the backseat, staring out at a plane that was disappearing quickly in the sky. Ashok merged onto the highway, periodically glancing at Nila through the rearview mirror. He wanted to break the silence to help his wife get out of her slump, but waited for the right opportunity.

"Ashok, why are some people followed by storms of disaster wherever they go, no matter how hard they try to avoid 'em?"

"It's all fate, dear. Though I truly don't understand it, it seems bad things happen to good people all the time. Life seems to be brutal to them. It is indeed unfair, Nila, you know? The good thing is they have the inner strength to overcome hard realities, to come out without faltering."

Nila closed her eyes, took deep breaths and exhaled slowly, pushing all the air into her burnt brain cells in an effort to rejuvenate them—a calming technique she learned from a yoga class she attended. Ashok watched her fall into a subdued state; calmness took over on her face. She began to swim through narrow tunnels and lanes of memory, picking the colors to paint the canvas of her friendship with Maya.

When she opened them again, they were at little Aparna's first birthday party, Ashok's colleague, Anand's, daughter. When they joined the party, the ballroom was overwhelming. The whole place was bursting with energy, with loud *Bollywood* music and the super-sugared kids running around playing tag.

The cheerful, charming girl in glittering *Ghagra choli* got Nila's immediate attention. She stood under the shimmering disco lights beside the skillfully crafted balloon rainbow. It covered the whole back wall. *Beautiful face!* The blue dress embroidered with silver threads and fringed in gold on her curvaceous frame gave her the stunning look of a diva.

"Who is that pretty girl, Ashok? Haven't seen her before…"

"Oh… don't you know her? That is Maya. The guy next to her in the long white *kurta* and blue jeans is Jamal, her husband, a computer consultant. They came on an H-1B work visa last month. He works with Anand at the same client site."

"Really? Jamal and Maya! Huh. Quite a match!" Nila arched her brows and made a funny face.

"They are no ordinary couple. They were followed in the Indian media for a while. I will tell you later."

"Very interesting." Ashok walked towards his friends, gathered near the snack bar, to chat. Nila glanced at Maya, then smiled. She, in return, waved her hands and walked toward Nila to introduce herself.

In a soft and friendly voice: "I am Maya, we haven't met before."

Nila hunched over a bit, "Hello… I am Nila."

They opted for a corner table to avoid the noise and the children who were running around like puppies let out of a kennel. It was a meeting of two women in a foreign country on a dependent visa, a status that forced them to be faceless in a big world of loneliness and restrictions. While their husbands worked, they shrunk within the walls of their apartments. The law gave them the status "dependent," a dependent on the spouse for everything. They had much in common, plenty to share. The long, boring days, once their husbands went to work, were the same. The chores were the same. They even saw the same dreams. The shapeless clouds floating over their skies cast the same perplexing shadows. They were mirror images that had never met.

"Maya, I feel we are like two sides of the same coin, minted, with tails on both sides by fate," Nila said, laughing as she sipped a bubbling ice-cold 7-UP, almost choking herself. Maya laughed too; for her, it was a big relief to find someone like Nila to talk to. The joyous moment brought both to tears at the same time. They looked away toward the babbling crowd, wiping the tears that were in a hurry to spill. Maybe they thought it odd to show their tears on a happy face. But for sure, it was the beginning of a true friendship; someone to share sorrow and joy in a place far from home. That relationship eventually gave them both the feeling of finding a sister and a friend.

On weekdays, when the husbands were at work, they engaged in long telephone conversations. There was nothing they didn't know about each other. When they had nothing to say, they left the phone on "speaker" and continued with their chores. It seemed to give them the feeling that they were not alone, that they were there for each other even if not together. Some days, Ashok dropped Nila at Maya's apartment; sometimes it was a trip to the shopping mall if he was able to take a quick break from work.

Maya and Jamal met in the city of Bangalore, the Silicon Valley of India, a city crammed with multinational software companies and computer professionals. Maya worked as a recruiter for a reputable information technology outsourcing company, where Jamal was a computer programmer. They were good friends. Like everyone else, they blended into the beats and colors of the metropolis without any reservations. For Maya, being part of a traditional, orthodox Hindu family from a small town in southern India, a city like Bangalore was a new domain for discoveries and experiences. She wanted to explore its captivating vigor and the beauty of its profound history. Jamal, a Muslim from the city of Lucknow in northern India, had similar interests but had grown up in an entirely different environment. Maybe they were fascinated by the differences between them, blinding them to all the rudiments of norms imposed by each of their communities. They were inseparable.

They enjoyed exploring the intricacies of Bangalore by going into the villages and taking part in the events and carnivals. They felt like part of a city where different ideas, beliefs, and ways of lives merged together. The glitter of the city lights never dimmed their feelings for belonging and their differences in religious beliefs. Whenever possible, they immersed themselves in the celebrations that made the streets crowded, colorful and noisy. They always looked forward to the *Chaitra*, the first month of the Hindu calendar, to celebrate *Karaga*, celebrations commemorating the goddess Adi Shakti's visit to Earth to bless her devotees. Without any hesitation, Jamal joined the local men, the warrior dancers dressed as females and bearing the tall floral pyramid balancing atop their heads. They hoped Adi Shakti, the goddess of universal energy, would be there for them always, giving them strength to withstand every adversity and menace the future could bring.

The influx of globalization had smeared the smoke of uproar all over and never settled. The country was going through a rapid cultural transformation, as no one had the patience to wait for the short-term turbulence to settle. The tug of war was between the overpowering new generation, who had conveniently forgotten their past and adapted to the western pop culture, versus the traditionalists that feared their centuries of culture being blown away in the western wind. Religious hardliners supported the fundamentalists, called this a historical juncture, and took over the moral policing. City centers and college campuses were targeted with violence to enforce their codes of conduct.

A few months later, it was Valentine's Day. Maya and Jamal were sitting outside a coffee shop, sipping spicy *masala chai* and nibbling on vegetable cutlets. The area was filled with couples professing their love and celebrating friendship. Soon a splinter group, claiming to be members of an extremist Hindu party, rushed toward them and circled, screaming, "Valentine's Day is against our culture. It is obscene and against our tradition."

A stout, ruthless woman pulled Maya down to the floor, kicked her, and said smugly, "If you are married you should have *sindoor* on your forehead." The men beat Jamal until blood seeped from him. They were both made to stand in the middle of the street and forced to do fifty sit-ups while holding their ears with criss-crossed hands. Pausing to watch the demeaning act, the traffic did nothing but continue to flow.

To make matters worse, some from the on looking crowd spread the videos of the incident through their mobile phones. The news media and the internet portrayed Jamal and Maya as heroes of the new wave of change. They became the paradigm for a new generation that is beyond caste and creed that suppressed progress for centuries.

The photo of the incident was reported on the front page of leading newspapers. In no time, it reached Maya's parents. Their daughter going around with a Muslim boy was a disgrace to the family. They were nervous and spiteful. Her family would rather she be dead than risk their honor. Soon they decided to stop the relationship at any cost. Steaming in arrogance, the family failed to understand the mindset and accept her freedom. Maya's family planned to make every effort to bring her under their control.

Maya's brothers and their family's henchmen, who came to Bangalore by surprise, couldn't stop the couple from becoming one at the government registrar's office. Their friends and other social activists formed a barrier to protect the newlyweds. The disillusioned family quickly conducted the rituals to disown her, protecting themselves and the family's honor from the anger of the community. It didn't stop there. The leaders of a Hindu funda-mentalist group alleged this as a planned "Love Jihad," where non-Muslim girls were targeted by Muslim men for conversion to Islam by feigning love. They even set a bounty on the couple's heads, a tactic of intimidation to spread fear among the youth.

Meanwhile, Jamal kept receiving threatening notes from a banned Islamic group that operated underground. A Muslim having a non-Muslim wife infuriated them. They vowed no peace for the rest of the couple's life until the girl converted to Islam.

Their apartment in Bangalore was vandalized. The outside walls were covered with hate messages and threats.

The awestruck couple stayed away from home. Evenings they hung out in public places and retreated to friends' homes who took turns providing refuge for them.

"Maya, how long can we live like this? Our friends… how long can they take this?"

"Jamal, I have scheduled a meeting with the HR Manager; hopefully he will give us some options, maybe post us in a quiet part of the country."

The hurricane devastating their life soon passed. News of Jamal getting an H-1B visa to work in the United States couldn't have reached them at a better time. They felt their prayers had been answered. Maybe there has been an accord reached between the Hindu and the Muslim gods, to let them be the butterflies in the garden blooming with vibrant dreams. They wanted to hover over the dancing daffodils and lilies, sipping the gushing nectar of freedom, without fearing the invading dragonflies.

Their last few days in Bangalore were unforgettable to them as they inhaled the mystic air of tranquility, anticipating life in a fenceless world. An escape to the land of freedom and opportunity thrilled them. Maya read about the place where they were going to begin a new life.

～♦

EARLY IN THE morning on Friday, September 15th, when the KLM 747 flight slowly rumbled down through the runway at the Bangalore International Airport, Jamal held Maya's hand and looked into her eyes. Gently he lifted and pressed her hand to his heart. She could feel its heavy drumming. He had the smile of a child seeing the most coveted toy among his birthday gifts. A sudden jerk and the flight took off into the air with them. They looked down through the window at the fading city lights and said together, "Goodbye Bangalore!"

When his heart went back to its normal rhythm, he said, "You know, Maya, I knew God would never desert us. He doesn't care where we go to pray. It is the evil within man that sees differences."

"Jamal, you are the sweetest and most innocent person I have ever met in my life. I love you more than ever. We have left all our troubles behind us. Don't worry too much. We will face everything together with courage."

～

DISPLEASED WITH THE slowing traffic, Ashok pushed the brake in irritation and turned the headlights on. "It's so dark, looks like there is going to be a second wave of the storm." Having no response from Nila, he turned back and had a quick peek at her. She still had her eyes closed, but her face looked eager, beaming a pleasant grin.

The airport... saying goodbye... it was heartbreaking. Hopefully, she is dreaming of something nice for a change! he thought. He didn't know Nila was welcoming Maya and Jamal to the US in her thoughts, a happy episode at the end of an exodus from peril.

～

THE EARLY FALL was picturesque in Minneapolis. Fresh air and the transcending soft, cool breeze in the new place gave Maya startling vigor. She spent time sitting on the apartment balcony watching the trees change colors.

Red, purple, yellow... Wow! It's so beautiful. Maya thought this must be what heaven is like, and she wished the leaves could stay like that forever. When the night sprinkled jewels in the sky, she watched those leaves blushing to the kisses of the entrancing moonlight.

The lovebirds quickly forgot their difficult past as they breathed the fresh air of their newfound freedom. In the wings of their dreams, Jamal and Maya flew above the migrating birds that were making golden lines in the blue sky. They enjoyed long walks along the trails around the beautiful lakes as they discussed their future plans. Sitting on the banks of the Mississippi, they listened to the song its waters hummed for them.

When Jamal was off to work in the morning, Maya walked to the Japanese garden across the street, adjacent to the community college. She dipped her feet in the cascading waterfalls that had been arranged to look like wild falls in a mountain valley. The sight and sound of flowing water made her lose track of time. She was lost in the pristine water's reflection of the garden's graceful red-striped pagoda. While standing on the red, wooden bridge, she flirted with the goldfish that were making synchronized moves to get her attention.

The gorgeous fall first lures everyone to dream beyond the mountains that touch the blue skies, but then disappoints. Maya watched the dead leaves falling one by one, making the trees stand naked and swing to the tunes of the gusty wind that turned harsher and harsher as days passed. The brilliance of the night sky had faded. The nights began to fill with shadows of thick gray clouds forcing the stars to take cover behind them.

⁓

FOR JAMAL, THE first week at work was very exciting. Working for a client, a world leader in the financial industry, was a dream for him.

"This will bolster my resume and career. I will be very marketable," he told Maya with pride.

The outsourcing company's office space within the client site was set up to have the same look and feel as the Bangalore office. The cubes were tiny and the open areas were cramped with seated programmers, similar to a call center. Ninety-five percent of the team members were from India, and many of them he had known beforehand. The management team did their best to maintain the same office culture as that of India. It assured the smooth blending of the stream of programmers who were coming and going, and quickly maximized productivity.

Jamal's immediate manager, Prem Shankar was an old friend and former colleague. In fact, they had both joined the company in Bangalore on the same day, but Prem had climbed the corporate ladder very fast. His managers praised him saying, "Prem has the right skills to be successful." But the rumor among the programming worker bees was that *Prem, the smooth talker, makes you feel like you are his best friend. If you turn out to be a threat to his career growth, he will stab you in the back.*

After a few days, Jamal came home late night after night. This was just the beginning. After that, he seldom came home for dinner on time and rarely had much time to stay at home on weekends. On the few occasions that he came home early, he was glued to the computer, remotely logged into work, monitoring the progress of the database updates. Every other night, he had to support the offshore team in India that developed some of their software, leaving him with less and less sleep.

This sudden change in her dreamy life disturbed Maya; it was like an unwelcome storm on a peaceful ocean. Fun trips and parties quickly vanished from their life. There was no time for anything after Jamal came home from work. The only consolation for Maya was the phone calls and occasional visits from Nila.

Extremely concerned, Maya asked, "Jamal, what's the deal? Isn't there any law that limits work hours? Maybe you should talk to Prem and get put on a different team. I am really worried."

"No, Maya. I don't think that will do any good. Asking Prem will hurt us more than help us. We are just high-tech slaves, chained to the work computer."

"It's wrong to treat people like this, Jamal."

"What options do we have, Maya? If I express my discomfort, they will cancel my visa and send us back to India. They know the game well. They play it perfectly. We are like the ball. We just get kicked around as they score bigger and bigger."

"So, do they treat everyone on the team the same way?"

"No, this happens only to people on visa. Everyone else comes at 8:00 and goes home at 4:00. Sometimes, to please the management, we are forced to complete the other's tasks, too. If they stay late, they have to be paid overtime. It seems the laws here are not to protect us but to punish us."

"I really feel you should try to join an American company."

"I checked about that with others in our team already. It is extremely difficult. They made us sign the contracts in India. Their lawyers will rip us apart with legal notices and lawsuits. They will make sure we don't get a job even in India if we abscond."

Disheartened, Jamal desperately looked for a trustworthy advisor to weigh his options in the current precarious situation. A few of his close friends, including Anand, had recommended Raju Varghese, a very friendly and sincere man, for honest advice. Anand had said, "Raju knows the tricks and trades of surviving in any work environment. He is a veteran! He's one of the senior most programmers in their group and is on the fifth year of his H-1B visa. He has survived many clients and managers." Though Jamal hadn't interacted much with Raju, he liked his personality. He always looked relaxed and never lost the grin on his face.

Someone mentioned that he had been that way since childhood. He maintained his smile and composure even if every system at their client site came to a halt at the same moment; even when there was no solution to the biggest problems, they attempted to resolve it.

Jamal waited for an opportunity to discuss his issues with Raju. Unfortunately, his cubicle was right in front of Prem's office. A confidential discussion was impossible around there, as it was always swamped with Prem's chums. He drafted an email to Raju, detailing his problems, but then dropped the idea out of fear—Prem monitored everyone's email inboxes. Instead, he printed the email and decided to hand it over to Raju when the time was right.

On a Friday evening, while working late, he stumbled upon Raju Varghese in the office break room. Jamal was excited to see him.

"Hi, Raju, I was looking forward to talking to you. It's for an opinion on my current situation. I hope that's OK."

"By all means, Jamal, I would be more than glad to help you in whatever way I can."

"I have printed out my situation and questions. I will drop it by your desk. Please let me know when you have a few minutes. We can walk and talk."

"No problem."

Almost a week had passed, but Raju hadn't responded yet. Jamal was nervous. Why is it taking Raju this long to respond? He saw Raju going to lunch with Prem. *Did he share the document with Prem?*

Maybe they are laughing at my problems while they sit at the Mongolian BBQ.

He couldn't imagine the consequences if Prem came to know about the document. But Prem didn't show any signs and was extremely friendly after he came back from lunch. Paranoid and restless, Jamal looked for clues of which way the wind blew.

"Knock knock."

"Hi, Raju. What a surprise!"

"Jamal, you want to go for a quick walk and grab a coffee? I have some free time now."

"Sure!"

They took the elevator to the lobby and strolled toward Caribou Coffee.

Jamal listened closely to Raju while sipping the double shot of the terribly bitter latte with his jaw clenched tight.

"Jamal, I can understand your situation very well. Things will get better once you get used to it around here, and readjust your expectations. Have patience and opportunities will pop up. This is a great country with a great system. If you follow the rules and work hard, anything is possible."

"Thanks, Raju, for your kind words."

"No problem, Jamal!" Raju said. "Also, let me tell you some unwritten laws in high-tech sweatshops like ours. Keep a note: it will serve as a survival guide, even though it may sound a bit funny."

Raju went on. "You are at your desk before the boss comes. You leave home only after you complete every task, and never before he leaves. There is no difference between weekdays or weekends, only delivery dates and release dates. Even in your dreams, never think you can fool your boss; you will be caught with your pants down. He is a master manipulator. If you are late to work and try to sneak in, don't be surprised to see him in your cube. Never say 'no' to your boss, he thinks it is 'yes.' You are entitled to take a vacation as per US labor laws, but you have to make up those hours and bill the client in advance. You can't trust anyone around you; they are all spies working against you, reporting to your boss for their own promotion. Your company will motivate you by promising a green card before your visa expires, but it will never happen." Raju paused for few minutes and got up. They both walked out of the coffee shop smiling, but Jamal's smile was dampened in sorrow.

He was like a traveler lost in the desert, praying frantically to find a drop of water before last breath. Then, whether it was real or a delusion, he saw the rain cloud hovering over, ready to drench him, lifting his spirits from the grit beneath. News of Maya expecting a baby made them forget about all their problems for awhile, drawing them into a new season of their life, a season of hopes blended with pleasant thoughts. They just wanted to live and dream in the moments to come, erasing the past.

Not much bothered by Jamal's hectic work schedule anymore, Maya kept busy filling the baby journal. She engraved her feelings as little songs for the baby growing within her, often singing them as lullabies as she stroked her tummy and her words reverberate like the chords of their bond. Some days she used colored pencils to draw pictures on the baby journal's blank pages. To her they were pictures her baby wanted her to draw. The smiling sun playing with grasshoppers on the lawn, the moon as an angel, holding her baby, surrounded by stars and all the other apparitions she saw while looking at the night sky.

Even as he stared at the dull sky, the thought of becoming a father overwhelmed Jamal with joy. He wished the silver streaks drawn in the sky for him would become wider and wider, purging everything else. When Prem was out of the office or in long client meetings, Jamal snuck out to listen to the babbling and feel the baby kicks on his face while the baby wiggled away in Maya's belly. Together, Jamal and Maya dreamed of playing with the baby. Dreams grew along with the baby in Maya's womb.

When the baby was sleeping inside her, or listening to Mozart through the headphones on her stomach, Maya and Jamal silently wrote potential names for the baby. Should it be a Hindu name or a Muslim name? How do they want their child to be raised? Who would be the guiding light, Lord Vishnu or Allah? As each day passed, their excitement brimmed over. They let their questions rest in time's chest to decide for later.

The due date was fast approaching. The doctor said it could happen any day. They both were ready. They double-checked the checklists, followed the instructions from the doctor's office, and practiced the breathing techniques from the Lamaze class.

On a Friday afternoon, Jamal was walking quickly towards the office exit, hiding his lunch bag.

"Hey, Jamal!"

He saw Prem with a sly grin, emerging from the conference room across the hallway.

"Not feeling well? Leaving early?" he asked in a singsong voice.

"Prem, my wife is close to her due date and has started to have pain. She is a bit worried; I just wanted to go and have a quick check."

"Really! I am so happy for you, Jamal. Somehow, I thought it was next month. Isn't her mom coming to help?"

"No. We have some friends who are helping us."

"That is great to have friends like that. But friends have limitations. You should try to do what everyone else does. Bring her mother from India. She will take care of everything, and you can stay away from doing all the baby stuff… if you know what I mean."

Yes! I know exactly what you mean. You want me to be at work 24/7 and not be mired down by family stuff. Jamal wanted to explode but controlled his resentment. He felt like a hungry animal in confinement waiting, at the mercy of the trainer, waiting desperately for a scrap of food.

"Yes, we are looking into it seriously," Jamal said in a hurry.

"Don't worry about the pain; it's a false alarm. You know, most women are very anxious and can barely handle the pain of a mosquito bite. Just the thought of a flu shot makes them faint." Prem laughed loudly, walking beside Jamal and continued along with Jamal outside the door and continued talking.

"You know, Jamal, I, too, want a baby, desperately, but my wife wants to wait till she gets her next promotion. A stable job and a good income is a must to raise a child. I was reading an article on *Forbes*. It costs $300K to raise a child from infancy to age 18. This doesn't include college expenses."

"Unbelievable!" Jamal said in surprise.

"It won't be a bad idea to send your baby to India 'til you get your green card."

"Definitely, we will look into that option."

"By the way, don't forget to come early on Sunday, our project's go-live day. All our hard work for the past year will be tested. I hope the software application launch goes smoothly. Also, I have recommended your name to upper management for a promotion. You are doing a tremendous job! Keep up the good work."

"Thank you, Prem, for considering me. It could not have come at a better time."

"You know, Jamal; more responsibility comes with more power." They both laughed. Jamal rushed home, feeling no remorse for the delay, but was glad for the promising conversation he had.

It was around 8 o'clock Sunday morning. Jamal was about to leave to work on the critical go-live of their project when he heard the loud cry that he had been dreading.

"Jamal, I am going to have the baby soon. Please, please don't go to work."

"Relax, Maya! Everything will be all right. Let's go to the hospital quickly."

On the way to the hospital, through the rearview mirror, he watched his wife in pain. Even on the brink of a nervous breakdown, his wife's face glowed in anticipation of the beautiful moments to come.

"Honey, just a bit more..." He tried his best to calm her down, forgetting everything else. For a while, only his wife and the unborn baby existed in his thoughts, not himself or his problems. He wanted to go beyond the speed his fifteen-year old car could handle. He even found fault with the light breeze, resisting his car's speed and wished it blew in his direction. He took the street's shoulder to pass the slow-moving Sunday morning traffic.

"Honey, in case we get pulled over, just cry loud. Seeing your situation, the cop will let us go."

He was ready to face anything waiting for him, but his subconscious was in the grip of something else, and the 9:00 AM mandatory attendance requirement at the office flashed before him.

He pulled out his phone.

"Ashok, can you and Nila come to the hospital? We are on our way."

"Oh! Sure, we will be there in a few minutes. Bye!"

The work pressure was mounting on him. He wished the baby had come a few days later. He pushed the wheelchair quickly through the hospital emergency door.

"Go straight. The elevator is on the left. Then go to the second floor," the volunteer at the entrance guided him. On his way, he constantly glanced at his watch. *Half past eight!*

By the time Nila and Ashok came, it was a quarter to nine, Maya was in the room, and all devices were hooked to the monitor. The beeps and clicks gave Jamal a headache.

"Hey guys, I need to be at work at 9:00 AM. I will show my face and will be back immediately."

By the time Jamal reached work, it was five minutes past nine.

"Hi, Jamal, we were all waiting for you. We expected you to be a few minutes earlier," an anxious Prem said.

"Prem, my wife is in labor. Can I complete my tasks and leave quickly?"

"Come on, Jamal… don't worry, hospitals here are really good. They will take care of her and the baby really well. You don't really need to be there. Think about it like you are in India. They never let men in the delivery room there."

When Maya was pushing to deliver the baby, Jamal was busy pushing deliverables for Prem's biggest release of the year, meeting the deadline and adhering to every specification. He silenced his mobile phone, which was ringing nonstop. With uncontrollable sorrow over his worthlessness, he stared at the computer screen that was spitting reports and error codes onto his face. He struggled to keep up, wiping the tears flowing down his cheeks, forgetting to apply the breathing techniques he had learned at the birthing class. They would have come in handy at that moment.

It was around 12:00 AM when Maya had their baby girl. Nila cut the umbilical cord in the absence of the father. The baby didn't cry for a few minutes, which worried the doctor. Maybe she was like her mom, holding all her sorrows to herself. Then little Ameera, lying on her mother's chest, looked into her mom's eyes and together they both cried for a long time. The cry gave joy to everyone else in the room.

Knowing that he wasn't there when he was needed most nearly drowned Jamal in shame. He slowly sank into the world where darkness concealed the daylight. The pain from life sliced through the dreams he saw with Maya, and it no longer meant anything to him. Life's bitter experiences that made him ride through the emotional roller-coaster over and over had to pay its toll. He became sensitive to little things and got frustrated. He began to have problems with everyone around him. At home, he sat emotionless, staring at his child for hours. He was a dead man living in a world of ghosts. Prem had a closed-door meeting with him after Jamal's sudden outburst at a client and his tardiness in attending the mandatory meetings.

Maya thought all his problems were work-related: stress and lack of sleep. It seemed all her worries had melted away with the baby's arrival. She ignored the changes in Jamal. Her life was centered on little Ameera, dancing to the tunes of the lullabies that filled the apartment walls.

Jamal was not the same person who boarded the flight from Bangalore and landed in Minneapolis on that chilly September morning. His mind, once filled with hopes and full of dreams, had become hollow. His heart, once filled with deep love for his family, had filled with hatred for himself. The stress in him was ballooning day by day. He was unable to sleep and unable to control his mind. He was living in a different world, with a mind lost somewhere in which he could not return.

It was on a Sunday afternoon. The baby had colic and was crying hysterically.

"Can you keep the baby's voice down? I am trying to get some sleep!" Jamal, taking a nap on the couch, screamed. Maya was shaken and upset to hear this from a soft-spoken guy like him.

"Sorry, Jamal, I will take the baby outside for a walk." She closed the door and pushed the stroller toward the walking trail.

After an hour in the stroller, the baby fell asleep. Maya returned to the apartment, opening the door quietly. Jamal was not asleep on the couch. *Maybe he has gone back to work,* she thought. She grabbed the sleeping baby from the stroller and walked toward the crib in the bedroom.

Maya screamed.

"Why did you do this, why did you do this, why did you—"

Maya fainted, falling sideways as she held the baby close to her chest.

Jamal had hanged himself, had succumbed to the miseries of life and surrendered to fate. The ceiling fan, unable to support the weight of the man, had fallen to the floor, covering his lifeless body.

~

MAYA AND NILA sat nervously beside Ashok while the immigration attorney glanced over the papers. She was a well-mannered, elegant woman in her fifties. The local chapter of a human rights group recommended her. Her posture, her wide brown eyes, and her sculpted face displayed confidence and self-esteem. She nodded, slightly arching her brows. Nila noticed the sudden change on the attorney's face. Nila massaged her twitching nose and attempted to relax.

"I am so sorry to hear about your husband. It is really an unfortunate situation." She took a deep breath and continued.

"Your visa status is that of a dependent. When the H-1B visa holder loses their job, in your case by death, the dependent is out of status. This means that you have to leave the country within a few weeks, as you will no longer be considered a legal resident."

"But, she has a life-threatening situation in India and a child born here, a US citizen. Is there any other option so she can stay here? She can live with us," Nila said in haste and gripped in the peak of her nervousness.

"See, there are provisions for political asylum and amnesty in the law, but those will not work in her situation. Maya's situation of facing religious and communal violence is not covered, and it is extremely hard to prove, anyway. The child can sponsor the parents when she turns 18."

After a brief pause, she continued.

"With the current laws as they are, proceeding forward won't do much. Sorry. I wish I could do something to help."

During the final few days of her stay in the United States, Maya and her baby girl moved into Nila's apartment. It was extremely hard for her to live through the memories and pain, alone in the apartment that had made her a widow and her daughter father-less. But in the short span of those few days, Maya had trans-formed into a different person. Her mind became strong enough to withstand anything. She was determined to face her fate. The flower's petals had fallen away, and she was prepared to handle the pain from its thorns.

While Maya was preparing for her journey, Nila and Ashok contacted all their friends in the US to find a way to help her. A position as a nanny, for instance; anything that would help her avoid going back to face the storm in Bangalore.

Ashok was excited to break the news of an opportunity for Maya through a friend at his work.

"Maya, one of our close family friends owns a motel in Chicago. I talked to him about you. They are willing to help you out. You can stay with them or can be a roommate in a small apartment with some of the other female employees. They will pay you cash, and it is safe. There are millions of undocumented workers in this country. Eventually, some kind of amnesty will happen, and you can get a green card."

"Sorry, Ashok! I have had enough of everything. I don't want to be a burden for anyone or live in the shadows. I will fight and live in honor as long as I live. I will not regret my decision. We are going back." Maya was stubborn and determined. They didn't pursue anything further to keep her in the country, but Ashok and Nila made every moment with them beautiful and memorable.

~

ON THEIR WAY to the airport, they avoided talking or making eye contact with each other. Instead, they turned their attentions to amusing the baby. To create a better mood, hiding her sadness, Nila made a funny face and in a baby voice said, "We won't miss you, Maya, but we will miss this sweet little cutie-pie." They all laughed together and tried their best to freeze their smiles until they split, suppressing the pressure consuming them. As they approached the airport, the overcast sky above them was turning darker and darker, preparing for its final grand show. They all knew that, like them, the thickening clouds wouldn't be able to hold on much longer.

Wingless Angels are falling....
Innocent children in school.
Why I See sad dreams, and
then it happens.

Every night differs,
So are the dreams they bring.
The shades of the darkness
Add depth to its quiver.
Dark colors, light colors
They just create the mood.

Fuzzy figures and blurry faces,
Props and characters
Never wait to dissolve into memory.
But some faces linger
Even beyond the dreams.
Unknowing, unwary eyes keep searching for them.

Dreams are two-dimensional
A notch below reality.
You never know the time,
Or how long, it carries you.
But you always hear its tick
Like the tears dripping from a deserted tunnel.

Dreams don't wait for us
We can only wait for them
We breathe the ocean and the roses
It takes us to the mountains and the forest.
And when we dream to dream,
We are like the sand dune blocking the wind.

Dreams

WRAPPED IN A velvet blanket, Nila jolted awake. With her head resting on the headboard, she sat on her bed, lost in a vacuum of unconsciousness. Then the reality. She was panting. She feared her heart would burst open from the gush of pain. Thrusting her ribcage against her thighs, Nila breathed heavily to calm herself down.

Wingless angels are falling from the heavens.

Clouds are dripping blood.

"The dreams I never want to come true... Why do these bad dreams come to wake me up, drowning me in an ocean of guilt? Why me? Oh God, why me? Please spare me."

She believed the nightmares that woke her early in the morning signaled something bad was about to happen. That thought hardened more and more in her as she grew older. Nila sobbed and sobbed. The spilling tears failed to clear the dense fog building before her from the daunting memories.

Nila was only seven when she began to experience the dire influence of dreams. Faced with startling events that followed the lurid visions, its impact on her perceptions forced her mind to transform. When all her friends talked about their joyous dreams of princesses and toys, Nila was living the dreams, dreams that became bitter realities. A childhood overwhelmed in fear of dreams—a fear she had ever since.

Little Nila was very careful with what she listened to and involved herself with. She read only stories that were certain to bring good thoughts and dreams and believed excessive daydreaming would help keep the dreams away while she slept. Her mind was engaged with the animals from Aesop's fables, reflecting on the amusing stories of the ancient Indian court scholar Chanakya and the one thousand-paged *Arabian Nights* stories. Deliberately she stayed away from the evening prayer that included *Ramayana* recital, the narration of war and the bloodshed filled *Bhagavath Gheeta* by her grandmother. The thought of the headless warriors and the weeping Sita Devi under the captivity of the cruel ten-headed demon king, *Ravana,* invading her sleep, terrified Nila.

Now, shaking her head in frustration, Nila quickly wiped the sweat on her twitching nose. Her husband, Ashok, whenever he saw her nose twitching would say, "Nila, your nose is shivering like a guitar chord. A fool will probably kiss you today." Then he would hug her and kiss her squirming nose to cool her down.

With a hollow look in her eyes, Nila glanced at their large, framed wedding picture on the wall. "Ashok, I wish you were here. Why are you always away when I need you the most?" Tears poured down her cheeks, making sultry circles on the velvet-covered pillow.

Nila lifted the silenced phone to turn the ringer on. She was shocked to see two missed calls from Hari, her cousin in Dubai. He was the chief engineer for the construction of the tallest tower in the world.

Chained to the moment, Nila's mind swiftly journeyed through the remnants of the grating childhood memories. It was the night before the Onam term exam. She remembered her first awful dream and the agonizing days that followed. The whole family is waiting… enduring each moment in fear… like animals trapped in a forest fire. Onam, a season of festivity and joy, became a period of unforgettable grief.

It was much too late when Nila went to sleep after studying for the last day of the exams. She fell asleep quickly next to her sister on the straw mat spread on the floor. It was early morning when Nila heard the sound of footsteps shrouded in the heavy chime of anklets coming closer and closer. Quietly, she got up, listened to the sound, then slowly walked toward the door. The floor was wet, but she was warm. She opened the door to a night that gleamed with moonlight. Nila felt weightless and drifted like a feather in the wind by an overpowering force. She saw footprints on the cobblestones and then tiptoed toward them with eyes darting around. She placed her feet in the footprints that had the color and smell of blood. The blood-stained grass with footprints extended further through the rice fields in the direction of the hills across from her home. She took a few cautious steps when, suddenly, a big hole appeared before her.

"Amma!" Nila screamed, shaking everything in and around the room, waking everyone instantly. In few moments, the whole family gathered around her. Mortified and plagued with fear, Nila glanced at everyone with a sheepish grin.

"Everything alright, my child?" asked her father, Appa, in a faltering voice, followed by a deep sigh. Muthassi, her grandmother, comforted her with gentle strokes on her forehead and ran her fingers through the feathery black strands of her hair.

"See, my dear, this is why I always tell you, never miss the evening prayers. The chant praising Lord Rama and meditation on Lord Shiva will keep all the demons away. Those monsters are always on the lookout to scare fragile minds when sleeping. Beautiful young girls like you should be extremely careful." She held her close with her arm around Nila's shoulder. Nila looked at her like a baby bird knocked out of the nest.

"Come to my room to sleep, I will keep those demons away," Muthassi said. Everyone went back to sleep. Nila fell asleep hugging her grandmother.

～

THE FOLLOWING DAY after the final exam, Nila was surprised to see Aunt Revathi, her dad's youngest sister, waiting outside the school gate. From a distance, Nila could feel the tenseness in her aunt's face. She looked restless and kept pushing an irritating strand of hair back into place. Chaman, son of Cheruman Pulayan, the loyal servant of the family, was also accompanying her. He waited behind with a knife tucked in his waist on the side. He looked far more serious than he usually was.

A spark of fear spiraled through Nila's whole body. Revathi Aunt came running and hugged her. Nila could hear Aunt's heart drumming against her face. She touched Nila's quivering lip that was suppressing something her mind wanted to give away.

"Is everything all right, Aunt? Did something really bad happen?"

"Hurry up, my dear, we need to be home quickly, and hide in a safe place."

"Why?"

Teetering, Revathi Aunt pulled Nila's hand to hurry her, and then whispered, "Nila, walk fast, the Maoist Naxalites have attacked Uncle Raghavan. There is a rumor they are here to wipe out every landowner. Police think they have weapons they brought from China hiding in the hills. All the men are hiding. The police are very scared and cautious. They do not want to protect us. It is very risky to face them, even with their guns that can hit their target from a mile away. Oh my God, the Naxalites!"

Nila, on the brink of fainting, grabbed tight onto her aunt's wrist.

The five-minute walk home seemed never-ending. Tears spilled from Aunt Revathi's cheeks and kept falling like raindrops into Nila's hands. As they ran, they kept looking back to make sure Chaman was behind them.

"How is Uncle Raghavan?"

"He is in a stable condition but has lost a lot of blood. He was stabbed four times in the stomach." Gasping, Aunt took a deep breath and continued.

"Thank God, Cheruman Pulayan heard the loud cry and ran out of his shack to see Uncle Raghavan in a pool of blood in the rice field. If not for him being there, we would have lost Uncle."

"Did he see who did it?"

"He said he saw three men in red shirts and long pants with their faces covered in black cloth. He took a quick look into their eyes. They looked familiar, but he could not recognize them. They darted through the rice field and escaped." Nila kept looking sideways at Aunt Revathi's face, listening while she walked briskly.

"Even if people witness, they stay silent out of fear for their own life. These days it is awfully risky to speak the truth. The Naxalites kill their witnesses."

The Naxalites were believed to be funded and armed by forces outside the country to trigger instability. They often fueled disturbances, extorting landlords and randomly slaughtering people to cash in on fear. Portraying themselves as the saviors of the downtrodden and those exploited by the landlords, the Naxalites had won the silent support of the meager peasants. During the day, the assailants hid in the hills or the huts of the lenient farm workers. The informants from the village sent food and communicated messages through the women who went to pick firewood from the hills.

From a distance, Nila could sense the tension that consumed her ancestral home. The home always stood out like the one majestic elephant that made other pachyderms look tiny at the temple festival. Its tall roof and huge teak pillars had hunched over a bit in the current turbulence. Amma, her mom, was waiting impatiently at the gate with eyes glued on Nila. She came running to the mud road and hugged Nila, then walked with her to the portico, holding her wrist.

Nila quickly glanced at the visitors sitting in the portico. Those frowns targeting her displayed nothing but were mere gestures of dramatic sentiments. A longtime member of the legislative assembly of Kerala state, Shivarajan, MLA, was sitting on the wicker chair located in the middle of the room. The bogus Gandhi follower, adorned in a handwoven white *khaddar* shirt and *dhothi,* sat with crossed legs. Suddenly, he lurched forward displaying a false sincerity. Periodically, he wiped the sweat from his forehead with the tip of the tricolor shawl that hung around his neck. Next to him sat the head constable, Gopi Pillai, in his khaki uniform. His face was red and looked dangerously ferocious. He held the tobacco wrapped in betel leaf in his left hand, twiddling it with his thumb, waiting to crush it in his smutty mouth. Soon, tossing it into his mouth and chomping, Pillai yelled something unintelligible toward Chaman. To reduce the anger and avoid his slurs, Chaman covered himself behind the topless coconut tree that was home to many ring-necked parrots every season. Birds took turns laying eggs in its hollows and no predators scared them in their safe haven. Maybe Chaman hoped for the same.

Shivarajan, MLA scowled toward the side where all the women stood in reverence. With an artificial grief on his face, he said, "I will talk to the Central Minister and have the Central Reserve Police Force come from Delhi to camp here. They will wipe out these criminals for good. The leftist government here is useless; they seem to have some secret agreement with these scoundrels." He pulled off the shawl and shook it angrily in the air to display his dissatisfaction against the leftist government.

Nila looked at her Appa's face. He wanted to suppress his annoyance at the hypocrisy of the shady politician. Neither he nor the people had any respect for the MLA. Like a comet, he would come during election time with a mesmerizing smile. He showered the people with money and alcohol in an effort to buy votes from the poor and illiterate. There was a rumor that he owned a mansion in Trivandrum and a lucrative cardamom estate in Munnar Hill Station, both obtained illegitimately.

Head Constable Gopi Pillai, with a silly grin, glanced at the women. The women avoided contact; they knew who he was—a womanizer. Some gazed at the worn-out mosaic floor to find newly emerging patterns and figures. Others stared at the distant hill that stood aloof, snubbing their family crisis.

Shivarajan, slanting his face towards Appa, continued. "Our people cannot live in fear forever. We are warriors. Let's take up weapons even if we are non-violent Gandhi followers. Our fore-fathers have fought wars and given up their lives for the people and the country. We will hunt down these traitors to char them in public." He gasped while his voice rose to a shriek.

Nila stood in front of her mother, holding onto her hands that were wrapped around her chest tightly. Nila knew she was becoming a stress reliever for her mom. She nudged her mom against the wall, wiggling when she tightened her grip to press her daughter closer to her. Nila constantly tapped her foot, watching people in the room and the hill like an oscillating pedestal fan.

Little Hari was lying on the floor sobbing. The crowd ignored his ever-present mumblings. Nila couldn't control her tears as she looked at his grief-stricken face. Quickly, she walked across the room and stood behind the door so that no one would see her tears.

Looking at Nila and her mom, the MLA asked with affection, "Sharada, your daughter is a big girl now. What's your name, child?"

"Nila!"

Gopi Pillai craned his neck, scanned the yard, and then gaped at Chaman standing next to the coconut tree.

"Why are you hiding there? Come here. Are you hiding some secrets, you dirty wretch?" he growled. "Do you know who stabbed Raghavan, your master? We know you folks are helping them, thankless creatures that you are."

With a trembling voice, Chaman mumbled, "We will never betray our master, Sir. Our life and body are enslaved to our master."

"You better not forget that when you see free-flowing liquor and money," Pillai said sarcastically, pausing for a moment and continuing to rage. "This land, always so peaceful. Look how it is now, thanks to the communists. They have caused this division. The lower castes who worked for the landowners have turned against their own masters. This is, indeed, the evil era. Who knows what will happen if we don't stop this nonsense? There was a time they were untouchable. Had to stay away from the public and their women were not allowed to cover their breasts in public. Our people fought and gave them freedom from this disgraceful life. Never let the camel's nose in."

Maybe MLA Shivarajan wanted to put a break on Pillai's attempt to distort history. He stood up from his seat. Those with the most basic knowledge of history know that, during a dark period in the history of Kerala, lower caste women were forbidden to cover their breasts unless they paid a tax based on the size of the breast. It was the valiant act of a woman named Nangeli who chopped off her breast and placed it on a banana leaf when the tax collectors approached her. Her death and the revolt from this incident forced this despicable practice to be abolished by the king.

"All right, we will do our best. Please don't hesitate to contact me. Raghavan is my brother too." He looked at everyone, and the MLA walked out. Gopi Pillai followed him.

⁓

THE PAIN NEVER ended. In fact, it was the beginning of many disasters to come for the family. Ten days of Onam holidays became unforgettable days of fear and sorrow. On the night before Onam, Uncle Raghavan's condition deteriorated with a severe fever. Organs failed. Soon his entire body turned purple. No injections or medicines could prolong his life.

Images of the last rituals of Uncle Raghavan flashed through Nila's frantic mind. Hari lighting the pyre, Uncle Raghavan's body covered in a white cloth. The fumes from it engulfed the whole village and kept the sun hidden for days. The dark clouds that hovered over their heads never let any ray of comfort penetrate. It rained for two days without a break, washing away the bloodstains that fell on the rice fields. Unable to bear the pain along with the betrayal from the land they once loved, Hari and his mom moved to Chennai to live with her brother.

A few days later, Police Constable Sukumaran came to visit Appa, wearing a khaki shirt and short pants and holding his baton, the baton thinner than his slender arms, for a weapon. He looked comical in his conical khaki cap with red crown. Sukumaran and his mother lived off of Nila's family, doing household work for them until he got the police job. All his childhood was spent lingering around their kitchen and yard. Appa was sitting on the armchair scanning the newspaper.

"Suku… I am glad you found some time to visit us. How are you?"

Sukumaran reverently came close to Appa and bowed his head with palms clasped together on the chest.

"Master… we know who did this heinous deed. It's the people who have worked in your land, whom you have fed. Vipers…bit the hands that fed."

Appa's chin dipped, then he shook his head in desperation. His eyes were moist. His veins turned thick and red. His manliness made him avoid eye contact as he fought back the tears. Still, Nila saw a teardrop roll down his cheek. Nila could hear his heart beat and saw his twitching nose from where she stood. She knew he always did this in an effort to cope with stress. She did the same.

Sukumaran let out a deep sigh, then sucked in a deep breath of air and continued. "I was asked to arrest and take the killers to the station. No one dares to do this for fear of their life. Some policemen even secretly support the movement. I've been a servant to this family forever and will be loyal 'til I drop dead. I am just a shoot that sprung up in this yard, breathing the air and feeding on the leftovers."

Sobbing, he continued. "I have two little girls, if something happens to me, my girls…. Master, if you say just one word… one word and I will go and get them." He stretched out his right hand and pressed himself against the wooden pillar and slowly sat down on the floor.

Appa bounced out of his chair, briskly wiped the sweat from his forehead with his fist and looked at the clearing sky to gather the strength to get him through the ordeal. Contemptuously, he laughed at his own helplessness and walked away without resentment. Nila could see the shadows of his sorrow swallowing the tiny hope he had left in him for justice.

Maybe it was his tears that melted God's heart. Or maybe it was the truth, which the helpless and the distressed don't need to tell God in the form of prayers. God did what man couldn't do by proving his love for every creature, good or evil, offering them the opportunities to mend. Later, in a major maneuver, the Central Police Force took over the area to cease the horrid activities. For the Naxalites, life in confinement for long years changed them for the better. They found time to read Scriptures. They listened and learned from other inmates, including some foreigners held for drug violations. With focused minds and repenting for their horrendous past, they explored the positive territories to open up their minds to new possibilities.

Many of them became evangelists and spent the remainder of their lives serving the less fortunate, tribal, and downtrodden ones as missionaries. One of the killers even made it to the national chess team, with fourteen years of training from a fellow inmate, a German national.

~

NILA SLOWLY GOT out of bed, phone in hand. She strolled toward the window then gently pulled open the blinds. She glanced up from her profound distress for the golden rays of the morning sun. But the floating images from her thoughts cast shadows on her vision. Nila dialed the number displayed on the phone.

"Hello… hello?"

"Hi Hari, it's me, Nila. Saw your missed call. What's going on in Dubai?"

"Everything is going great here."

"Are you still working on the tallest building in the world?"

"No, we've completed that project and moved on to another high-rise building project. Is everything all right there?"

"Yes. We are doing well, Hari."

"Nila… I just saw on TV… some school shooting in the US. A crazy person shot several little children. Just wanted to make sure all you guys are safe and everyone you know is all right."

"Oh… my God, I hadn't heard anything. I slept late and just got up. Let me turn the TV on."

Nila hurried into the living room and turned the TV on.

"Oh my God, my dream... is it real? Again! Or am I still in the dream?"

Angels stained in blood falling from the sky.

"Why is this happening…? Oh God, you are so cruel! Why these little angels?" With quivering lips, she blubbered.

With her head trembling and body shivering in weightlessness, Nila fell to the floor, like the angels in her dream, into the blazing fire of remorse. Through her puffy eyelids, she stared at the television as if nothing separated her from delusion. The images changed. She saw nothing but colorless pixels and grains dissolving into the elusive sky, where she stood helplessly watching the wingless angels falling. She wanted to cry. The petrified mind failed to invoke emotions, and her barren tear glands failed to comfort her with tears. When her senses came back to her with the images of agony, she could not take it anymore. She muted the TV and hated everything.

Every sound pierced her skull. Every image blinded her. It was just before noon when Ashok returned home. He unlocked the door and was surprised by the quietude. He missed the usual jingling anklets running towards the door.

"Nila, where are you? Did you hear about the—"

Seeing Nila, he was stilled for a few moments, with all his

muscles gone stiff and reflexes disappearing. Slowly, he regained his composure and scrambled to say something, but swallowed everything he wanted to say. *A wise decision* he thought, in a state of indecisiveness.

He had never seen Nila in such a devastated condition. The pale face and her eyes—staring into the gloomy sky outside the window. Strange silence gripped the whole apartment. He felt like he had suddenly landed in a domain unfamiliar to him.

"Nila, you all right, dear?" Baffled and restless, Ashok glanced at the TV for a few minutes. "So sad… some freak! Really unfortunate!"

Slowly he slid down to sit next to his wife. He wrapped his arms around her shoulders then squeezed her close to his chest and rested his face on hers.

"It's too sad; we can do nothing other than shed tears and feel sorry for everyone going through this tragedy."

"Yes, feeling sorry… I feel so helpless and sorry for myself, Ashok."

"Relax! Don't take these events too personally. Time will erase the pain and the bad memories. We have to go on with life hoping for the best."

"It is so easy for you," she exclaimed in a faltering voice. "I feel I am a burden to this world. It's my dreams. The ones that make me panic. My mind drowns in torment. Why do they come true to haunt me forever?"

Ashok put his hand over her shoulder and tried to console her. "Your dreams are just meaningless illusions churned in the folds of your brain, smearing fear into your thoughts when you fall asleep. They have nothing to do with you or reality. Don't fall prey to superstitions. Mere coincidence is drowning your mind in apprehension."

Nila, reduced to tears, said, "I don't know what I will see next,

Ashok. I really don't know what is going to happen next. I am too scared to sleep."

"I think you shouldn't watch any more TV." He took the remote control and turned the TV off, then sat on the couch and pulled her up.

"What you really need is to listen to some soothing music. Music that will make you forget everything. Rhythms and beats that will make you float in the waters of tranquility."

He held her shoulders and let her rest on his lap, then slowly stroked his fingers through the silky black strands of her hair. Nila closed her eyes, listened to the silence that she hadn't experienced for a very long time.

"Nila, do you remember the night we walked through the rice fields near your home? The full moon was so bright, and it was gleaming like it was day. You wanted to walk to the hill on the other side and wait on the rocks till the sun came out."

"Yeah..."

"In that light, we could see the green grasshoppers on the rice plants that swayed in the wind with shiny golden rice flowers. When that cool breeze made us shiver, we sat on the stepping-stone next to the tiny creek watching the red rosebuds bloom, for hours. Its virgin fragrance... Nila, can you smell it? Can you feel that breeze feathering your face, making your hair fly all over my face?"

"Yes, I can, yes I can..."

Slowly she drifted to sleep. Ashok wished she would dream of flowers and butterflies. He looked, with a smile, at her beautiful face like a master magician after completing his most risky feat.

THOUGH ASHOK NEVER telecommuted from home, on that Friday, he decided to do so with the intention of giving company to his grief-stricken wife. When it came to his wife, he did everything with precision but was always unnoticed by everyone.

"Honey, last month was so hectic at work. Let's have our friends over tomorrow. It's been a while since we had a party here. We'll order food and watch a movie. Do you know of any good movies?"

"I really don't know. Anything is okay with me, I guess," she said reluctantly.

By the time Ashok was back after picking up food and beer, half the gang had arrived. A few of the women were near the stove frying *samosas* and the others sitting at the dining table were chatting seriously about the latest Hindi movie releases and the super-hot gossip about the Indian movie stars. The men were counting the cards in anticipation of the late-night bridge game that would typically end by the daybreak.

"Hey, Ashok! Where were you, man? We were waiting and waiting for the spirit of happiness. Please pour upon us, brother," Thomas Chacko quipped, a Syrian Christian from *Kerala*. Bold and witty, Chacko was looked upon as a hero by all the men in the group. They believe he helped them venture out and enjoy the true freedom of America when they were newbies in the country. They always opened their hearts to praise him following a few rounds of drinks. How could they not? The braggart showed them the path to a truly American life. He showed them proper bar etiquette and the latest dance moves. He convinced the lifelong vegetarian Brahmins to feast on "vegetable-fed" organic chicken without guilt. He even helped them to integrate into society by suggesting they Americanize their names: from Krishna to Kris, Narayan to Ryan and Girish to Gary.

In spite of Ashok's warning to his friends to avoid talking

about the school shooting, no one seemed to listen to him. Once the alcohol took over their tongues, they couldn't bear that pain. They engaged in resolving the problems by brainstorming ideas to save the world.

"Unbelievable! Such a thing could happen only here in the US. Why can't they ban guns? Every week there is gun violence in the news. It is so sickening." Narayan, also known as "Ryan," feverishly said.

"Hey, Narayan, it is not as easy as you think. Thank God! This is not like India or other developing countries where corruption is clogging the system, choking progress. I don't think it could get more perfect than it is here. Have you ever had to bribe anyone here?"

"You are so right! Is there anyone who hasn't passed a bribe at a government office in India? Even to get a small favor done, you have to please even the walls and the pillars. What a polluted system. Too many leeches!" Girish said.

"Why blame just government officials? Look at the state governments there. They have no time to take care of the people but find the time to resolve their internal problems. The only ones benefiting are the super-rich and the Swiss Banks!" Chacko chuckled.

"I am not sure… but here things are not as perfect as you think. Corruption happens in a sophisticated way. Have you heard of big lobbies? They dictate major policies here. Politicians, when their political career decelerates, take up jobs or work as lobbyists for big bosses. Nothing is going to happen! As usual, people have no long-term memory. The media will move on to the next hot issue," Ryan said.

"Too bad nothing will change, what a tragedy for those families. Anyway, at least be glad we can talk about these issues and don't have to fear any postings on Facebook," Ashok said. Everyone laughed at the joke regarding the recent arrests in a major city for liking a social media post that criticized a communal party leader.

"Take a break from the international debate, dinner is ready!" announced one of the ladies. Everyone quickly gathered around the table, inhaling the hot *biryani* and the sizzling *samosas*.

SUNDAY MORNING, THE sun was high in the sky when the cuckoo clock in the living room woke Nila up. She counted: it cooed nine times. She curled onto the fluffy pillow hoping she could go back to sleep. She had no energy to get up. The short-lived aberrant night had punched her into weariness. She wished she could lie down like this forever. An elusive feeling came over her, her senses and body floating through a murky cold tunnel of hopelessness. That Ashok had gone to work on Sunday morning to take care of some business also upset her. She stared at the framed photo on the wall. The smiling faces of her mom and sister next to her dad. He was looking as if witnessing a wonder, with his eyeballs bulging under the arched brows. It was always a big challenge to get him to stand still for few moments.

She mumbled, "Mom, I wish you were here; I could just rest my head in your lap. You rubbing my forehead will clear my mind and the heaviness in my head."

Nila gathered all her energy and pushed herself to the edge of the bed, then looked at the colorful shadows shimmering on the window treatment. The silky material, hand-woven by some tribal settlers in her village, was bought on their last trip to India. She walked slowly, running it between her thumb and index fingers, then opened the blind.

"Oh, it's sunny and pleasant!" The bright blue sky made her squint. She quickly opened the window, letting the morning breeze bathe her bedroom to eliminate the lingering cloudiness. The breeze streaming through the naked trees rubbed her face. She breathed in the air that carried a nip of the blossoms to come.

She looked straight across the road at two towering churches. They faced each other like corner convenience stores, competing against each other to save the lost souls. Nila often wondered, "Why two churches? They have the same God and teachings." One looked old, with elegant stained glass all around it, boasting of its past with pride. Its bell tower with the marvelous peal reminded her of the old school and the nuns who walked around like penguins monitoring their activities. The other church looked very modern, like a spaceship emerging from the clouds peering toward the future. Both displayed entirely different views, raising unanswered questions in her curious mind.

Both churches' parking lots were busy with happy faces, hugging, and handshaking. Nila could feel the music of joy buzzing in the air. It was getting close to the top of the hour, and the parking lots were filling with cars. Men and women were disappearing into the buildings. People in coats and ties were filling the church's northwest corner. The other one had more of the casually dressed. *Maybe one is for the rich and the other for the rest,* she thought.

Nila always wanted to go and have a quick peek. She wanted to see the inside to find what they do on Sunday mornings that keeps them cheerful. *There has to be something that brings them together, week after week. How can the people be so happy and look so peaceful? Why can't I be happy like them and emerge from the gloom?* She remembered what her dad used to say, "Life is a rag that soaks all the joy and pain around it. Place it in the midst of joyous minds, and you can feel the power. Your fate is in your own hands."

The church bell from the St. Mary's Catholic Church woke her from her thoughts. She closed her eyes, imagined herself dissolving into that soul quenching accord. Her mind resonated with the replenishing reverberations. Nila inhaled the air that was scented in serenity. It scurried through her veins, quickly filling every cell with a new life, flushing her with grace. The inner strength that empowered her made the emptiness that besieged her vanish.

"I really need to do something to get out and break the bonds of fear forever."

Like a spring night breeze inundated with fragrance, her heart was filling with joy ready to sprinkle all around her. Nila got ready quickly, wearing her favorite pink and blue skirt and top. She looked in the mirror, stretched her lips to even out her favorite light pink lipstick.

"Yes, I look beautiful."

She locked the door and walked out of her apartment building. The wind under the gangly trees made her silky hair slither all over her face. The Sunday morning traffic was light. She crossed the street quickly to cut across the parking lot toward the newer church. Both the churches had already started their services. She heard the claps and the loud music from the parking lot itself.

Nervous, Nila gathered all her courage to walk into the church. A few people in the back rows turned toward her with grins and welcoming nods. A pleasant lady in a red dress came toward her, held Nila's arm, and whispered, "Hello there, welcome!" She led her to a seat next to hers. Nila's heart rate dropped to normal quickly, making her feel very comfortable. Despite the loud music and the loud clapping of hands, she could hear the woman ask, "What's your name?"

"Nila."

"Nila! Nice name. Today is the celebration of life. Just enjoy the service."

"Thank you!"

The music stopped and a formally dressed person came running down the aisle. He had the speed and energy of a cheetah.

"Praise the Lord!" he screamed.

"Amen!" everyone responded.

He repeated it three times, each time the volume soaring.

"What a week it was! Did you ever ask God, why did *this* happen? Why this to little kids? Why didn't you stop this from happening?"

He paused for a moment and looked into the eyes of the people sitting in the front rows. Then he continued, "Have you ever asked God why he made us smile when we are happy and cry when we are sad? Have you asked God why he made the night and the day? Let us thank God for giving us each other... each other to hold on... to share our pain and joy. Let us stand up and hold each other's shoulders and pray."

Nila looked around and stood up along with everyone else. They repeated with the pastor, "Thank you God for giving us each other, each other to strengthen our hearts, share our pain."

"Amen."

"Let us share our pain," he hollered. "Let us share our pain with each other. Give your pain to others and take their pain onto your shoulders to relieve them."

The loud music, drums, and the flowing, exuberant energy lifted Nila into a revelation, an experience unexplainable, leading her to an unknown state of mind. She shared her sorrows with people around her and then listened to theirs. She hugged everyone around her, giving her sorrows and pain to others.

Nila had the vibe and felt the power of sharing the pain, taking the pain together. *Living alone with a lonely heart is no longer an option for me,* she thought. She slowly walked out, then paused for a moment on the church steps in disbelief of what had happened to her. The world around her looked different than what she saw through her apartment window. The blue sky never looked so clear, not even a tiny hint of a dark cloud could be seen. She tread along the walkway, then cut across the freshly mown lawn toward her apartment. The grasshoppers and beetles slunk out of her way. She walked along without hurting anything. She felt like a soldier returning home after a war, a war that had lasted for years.

The low hanging branches of the cherry trees were brushing her hair. She pulled a branch toward her and felt the tiny buds sprouting on them. *Soon these branches will be covered with soft leaves, then they will cede to the alluring flower that will envelop all beneath, erasing everything from everyone's memory.* Nila felt the poet within her soul reemerging, a talent she discovered in the solitude of her mundane daily life. The smell of the first rain, the beauty of the blooming tulips, and the dew drops in the morning's golden rays that paint magnificence on the butterfly's wings, added colors to her colorless moments. When her mind wandered into the sweet childhood memories of running behind dreams in the rice fields, chasing the butterflies, making the dragonflies lift tiny rocks, and singing along with the early birds, she painted them into words radiating hopes and brilliance.

Like a free bird, she hummed and danced on her way home. She had never felt this happy and excited coming to the apartment. Sitting at the worktable, she looked into the world outside through the wide-open window for few moments. She pulled the gold-nib fountain pen from the holder and began to write. The beginning of her new life spilled onto the notepad as a song of healing and hope.

Some dreams, I never want to be awake.
I pray the night never ends, leaving the stars to shine forever.
Some dreams, I never want the day to break.
I know its tormenting moments would haunt me forever.

Some say the remnants of the past
Make joyous pearls in the brain folds for the present,
To me, it is the reflections of memories from the future
Breadcrumbs dropped, deceiving elusive realities to come

Wingless angels falling from the heavens
Drenching the clouds on its way in blood
Oceans merging in rages, submerging the mountains
Tears from the skies causing the rivers to flood

I'm just a thought; I'm lost in someone's mind
Gathering pain for unknown losses to come by
I drift in the wind, a sparrow amongst the dragons
Waiting to be swallowed by stark naked skies

My eyes, staring beyond the rain clouds to see the impending
My heart, a candle unnoticed, burns in the daylight,
My face leans forward, blending tears of last raindrops falling
I hear a whisper from within

You are not alone; foregone are the days forlorn
Pain in your soul will never wane
Together our hearts will beat for us to move on
Together we will share our grief and pain

While my ears listen to the song of comfort
Like the breeze that kisses to bloom the rose buds
My heart lingers to feel the feathers of tranquility
Angels circle above turning fallen wings to colorful clouds

A man in rags came to the junction.
He plays beautiful music with a flute.

Unable to hinder the magnificent glory,
Desolate clouds part in reluctance.
Stunned by the crimson carriages drawing
Night's agony fades to distance.
Rustling breeze hugs the fruitless
Easing the pain of barrenness
Blessed ones dance to the magic winds
Spills all over its enticing fragrance
Empty pews strain listening to unsung hymn
Stained shadows gasp to live another moment
Moth-eaten stumps began to dream
A new shoot, a new life, graceful and vibrant.

Neelan (The Blue Man)

H E WAS FILTHY and stunk like a water buffalo but, still, no one wanted him to be thrown out from the temple junction. The moment he placed his lips on the reed, the entire place paused for a bit before getting back to the routine.

"No one could ever play a flute like him; no one could ever play such divine melodies!" Some even believed he was the manifestation of Lord Krishna; even his physical appearance didn't change their perception. In fact, that was the only reason the police did nothing when the nearby shopkeepers and the influential bank manager, Jose Chandy, filed a complaint against Neelan for being a public nuisance. The police knew he was not breaking any laws or creating a traffic jam. "Just a nuisance for some... not all," they responded verbally. Then they reported that there is no enforceable law in the Indian Penal Code against someone previously determined by the court of law to be mentally unstable just for being a nuisance.

Everyone referred to him as Neelan (the blue man), the nickname for the blue-skinned god, Krishna, who plays the never-ending love songs to his fervent devotees. Like the god, he wore nothing above his waist except for the one-day-old garland, made out of marigolds and hibiscus. The temple priest tossed them away at the end of each day. He collected the garland before the rodents and the temple cows ruined it. The flowers on the garland didn't lose their fragrance for another day and suppressed the odor that engulfed him. On occasions, like exams and birthdays, some school girls threw jasmine ropes at him. He strapped them around his wrist. He always wore the same torn camouflage pants with both legs rolled up to his knees. Ex-military man, Narayanan, had gifted him the pants a while ago when he was going to the local police station to give a complaint. It was a petition to find Radha, his wife-to-be, who had gone missing. An ardent fighter against class wars and a silent supporter of local labor movements, Narayanan encouraged Neelan to wear them. He thought, *someone like Neelan, and all* Untouchables, *who slaved for a family for generations may get a bit of respect by ditching very informal* lungi, *a long piece of cloth wrapped around the waist, to the police station.* Wearing modern dress worn by Europeans and upper-class Indians really didn't work out for Neelan. Sub-Inspector George Joseph ridiculed him by saying "Did you run away from the circus? Go back and clean up elephant droppings."

Every morning when Kutty Chettan opened his stationary store, he squeezed a bit of blue fabric whitening dye into Neelan's palm. Neelan would rub it all over his chest and face in an effort to transform into Lord Krishna. After that, he tied a large lock of his severely matted hair on top of his head, mushroom-like, and placed a peacock feather over it. His remaining untied curly hair hung over the shoulder. On the sides, it blended with his grimy beard that had many strands twirled up like hooks that danced in the wind with his music.

Neelan stood on top of the raised stone wall at the left edge of the culvert at the intersection of the main road and the dirt road going towards the Kaipuzha stream. It passed through large stretches of rice fields that reached Vembanad Lake. Holding his reed like a statue, he remained there from morning to sunset, filling the junction with his melodies. When the bus stopped at the junction, passengers threw quarters and five *paisa* coins at Neelan's feet. He spoke to no one. He smiled at no one. He continued playing the reed. When he was hungry, he would stretch out his arm, staring at the glass window of St. Teresa's Hotel & Teashop. Proprietor Monachan gathered all the unsold snacks from the previous day into a newspaper cone and offered it to him. Neelan would bow at Monachan's generosity and walk back towards the culvert, staring into the cone. In a minute, he would hurriedly gulp down the meal, and continue with his course.

Beneath Neelan's feet, a conduit carried the runoff water from the temple pond leading it into to the Kaipuzha stream. Eventually, it discharged into the Meenichil River. Most of the year, it was dry. Shopkeepers threw their waste and rotten vegetables into it, attracting stray dogs and rats. Heavy rains caused flooding. There was a rumor that Neelan petted a large snake living in the drain below. The chatter got stronger when someone saw him approaching the milkman, Nanu, with an empty coconut shell in the early morning hours. For fear of snake bite and the uncertainty over Neelan's reaction, no one dared to seek the truth. Eventually, the rumor faded to an unproven whisper.

~

NILA AND HER friends were scared of Neelan. She never paused to listen to his charming music. They walked quickly past him on the opposite edge of the road when visiting the temple. Nila always felt Neelan had something brewing inside. His overgrown bushy eyebrows subdued his intense eyes—eyes that sat deep in their sockets... revealing nothing but observing everything. Despite her aversion and fear, she still kept the flute that her uncle, Anandan Mama, had gotten from Neelan; a gift to Nila when she expressed her interest in music. Neelan would go into the bamboo forest on the other side of the Meenichil River to collect reeds. He made flutes for children; handing them out to any who asked. When one of the local lads won a prize at the State School Arts Festival for playing a Neelan flute, people came from faraway places seeking their own flute. They all thought there was something special about the ones he crafted. The flutes sounded soft to the ears but were sharp enough to etch the melodies in the heart. The sound never left anyone and kept Neelan in everyone's thoughts. Nila believed that a piece of Neelan's soul was infused in every flute he made and it never would leave whether he was alive or dead. She derived philosophical reasons for the mysterious notes the flute played while she held the flute at an angle in the wind. Though she never wanted to think of him, she always kept her reed in her room in a place of reverence, next to the images of gods and goddesses.

At night, Neelan slept over the salt chest kept on the veranda of Kutty Chettan's shop. No one locked salt chests these days. Salt was worth next to nothing; not even worth stealing by the lowest thief.

Neelan was scared of police; he knew they were not his friends. He would disappear into the culvert when he heard the rumble of Sub-Inspector Mathew Jacob's Royal Enfield Bullet motorcycle from miles away. Neelan was too scared to make eye contact with the retired police constable Bhaskaran Nair. He trembled and his heart drummed wildly, even when the well-mannered retired police constable Nair was in the vicinity. Neelan knew he was harmless, yet he kept silent watching the truth being betrayed. Not for any reason would Neelan go near a policeman, especially if the officer was cruel. That was the only reason why no one ever thought of considering him as a suspect when Sub-Inspector Jacob was found dead in the bathroom... the victim of a snake bite. That day, people had seen Neelan riding on a water buffalo, steering with its horns near the Inspector's home. Imagining him capable of playing the role of *Yama-Raja,* the god of death, for the Sub-Inspector was absurd. That evening, Neelan bathed the buffalo in the creek. Later he took it to the butcher to have it slaughtered.

Following the funeral of SI Jacob, when the family distributed alms and rice porridge to the wretched, Neelan also stood in line. Among the large crowd of local laborers living in misery and toiling like slaves, the Inspector's wife noticed him and showed extreme compassion. She knew that his coming to receive the alms was an important gesture. It implied Neelan had forgiven her husband's callousness; the man could rest in peace. She had no doubt that Neelan was innocent, and her husband was aiding the culprit to escape by being cruel toward him. For Neelan, it didn't matter whose funeral it was; he was always hungry and showed up when the porridge was distributed.

After eating, he always left the place in haste. He knew she was innocent. The only mistake she had made was to marry the policeman; pre-arranged and beyond her control. From that day onward, he patrolled in front of her home in the middle of the night, making sure she was safe.

After the monsoon flood, the Public Prosecutor, Sivadasan, died from a snake bite while sitting in his office. No one said Neelan was behind that death. Why should a poor soul, one who had lost his mind, be suspected? He is capable of doing nothing but playing a flute. Everyone blamed the landslide in the Western Ghats that swept snakes into the area from the mountains and forests. Hysteria and fear of snakes spread when the wealthy landlord Joseph died. His wife saw an eight-foot cobra slithering away into the backyard and away from the house.

Neelan went to Joseph Muthalali's funeral. He called him 'Muthalali,' a title for one who is rich and powerful. He looked at Muthalali's fair face that had turned dark blue, like his own chest.

Like his blue face. His former Muthalali, the one who owned him, had become like him in death... another Neelan, a blue man. He cried loudly, unable to control himself.

"My master... my master... you've left us. Oh God, you left us. We have no one. Why did you leave us in such haste?"

Everyone watching him felt for him and his master. The women watching him sobbed and wiped their tears with the tips of their *sarees*. Soft-hearted ones covered their tear-filled eyes so no one would notice. Affluent men glorified the deceased for his good heart. They were impressed by his skill in being able to turn an enslaved wretch, even one out of his mind, into one who felt a sense of loss for his owner. Reverend Fr. Antony highlighted Joseph's compassion to the needy in his eulogy. A man showered, abundantly, love and compassion on the unfortunate and the exploited ones around him. The priest even went to the extent of comparing Joseph to Mother Teresa, the legendary nun who lived among the destitute in the slums of Calcutta.

NEELAN RAISED HOPE and lifted the spirits of those who were exploited. He was loved by his people but loathed by the ones who stood against them. He lived in a prejudicial system that was created based on the shade of light reflected on one's skin. For generations, these unfortunates toiled from dawn to dusk with heads down, faceless. Dreams meant nothing. They fought against their own will in the scorching sun. They grew the crops, they filled the granaries, but great misery and disgrace were what they received. When the labor-friendly leftist parties brought awareness of the rights of the most vulnerable group of people in Kerala, the working class gained the strength to question. The prior success of land reform legislation had boosted their morale.

Gaining strength from the movement, Neelan chose to question the norms and the unwritten laws society imposed. He demanded a wage to keep them from starving during the famine months. He strengthened the weak to rise against injustice and harassment toward their women. Landlords and the like couldn't accept the loss of the perks they enjoyed with dominance. They made no mistake and gave no leeway to those they controlled. Upset but devious, they waited patiently for their turn.

Everything turned upside down for Neelan when his wife-to-be, Radha, disappeared one evening. That whole day she had worked at Joseph Muthalali's granary. Muthalali's men spun rumors of her running away with a boy from the nearby village. Neelan knew she wouldn't do that, and he knew who was behind her disappearance. This had happened to many others, but their weakness kept them from reporting.

The transformative land reform ordinance that was passed into law by the State had its own trap. The poorest in the village, those who toiled for their daily bread, had also received a tiny slice of land on which to live and farm. But most of them were forced off by the shrewd ones like Joseph. When it didn't rain, all their crops died. When the drought came, they all fell into debt. Large tenants gobbled up the land for next to nothing; turning the prior owners into beggars. Soon Joseph became their *Muthalali*, the modern-day landlord. He owned almost all the fertile land in the region. Quickly he grew to be the wealthiest. His greed for wealth made him meaner and meaner with a diminishing heart. He slapped them when he was mad and slapped them more when he was happy. Joseph chose who would work on his farm and how much they got paid. He tossed out the ones he didn't like; they had to run away to faraway places to find work.

When the good-looking Radha went missing, everyone knew Muthalali was behind it. But no one dared to ask him, not even Neelan. The next day, Neelan approached C.L Rajan MLA, a member of the Legislative Assembly and the powerful stalwart of the ruling Congress party. He offered every help and promised to be at the police station. Neelan didn't know MLA was in Muthalali's secret payroll. That afternoon Neelan, accompanied by labor union leader Comrade Kumaran, went to the police station to give the complaint. Sub-Inspector Mathew Jacob ridiculed both and asked them to come back in a few days. That night, the humiliated Comrade organized a torch-lit protest in the main road from one edge of the village to the other. In the dark, everyone kept their faces away from the light, so Muthalali's men didn't take revenge on them. They raised their voices against Joseph Muthalali and the Police Sub-Inspector. Comrade took the opportunity to shout slogans against his arch-rival MLA Rajan, who had defeated him in the previous state assembly election.

It was more than six years ago, six years three months and fourteen days to be exact, since the death of Sub-Inspector Mathew Jacob from a snake bite. Coincidentally, it was the third day after Radha had gone missing. A few women on their way to work in the morning spotted her bloated body floating in the Kaipuzha river near the screw-pine bushes. Hearing the news, Neelan fainted. At the Medical College hospital, it was reported that Radha had been murdered—suffocated not drowned. That afternoon, just before the sun dipped below the horizon, everyone working in the field witnessed a sad scene—Neelan walking in handcuffs accompanied by two policemen. Everyone stood still, watching him disappear into the darkness.

At the police station, Sub-Inspector Mathew Jacob was waiting for him. Predatorily approaching, Jacob reached the petrified prey. Neelan prayed, hoping he wasn't as mean as he looked. The Sub-Inspector raised his heavy police boot and, with all his might, kicked Neelan squarely in the stomach. His limp body crashed against the blood-stained concrete wall. Neelan dropped on the floor like a dead fish. With an insolent smile, the Sub-Inspector stated, "So you did it!"

"No, sir, I didn't do it. It is—"

"Yes, you did it!" he screamed as he spat on his face and walked away. After a few minutes, two policemen came inside. They both were drunk. One of them poured a glass of ice water on Neelan's face. The floor was like glue, no matter how much he moved, he couldn't get up.

He looked at them and said, "I did nothing." The vicious policemen glanced at each other and laughed raucously. One of them had blood-red eyes and his fists tightened, ready to do his worst. The other policeman twirled the tip of his mustache. Neelan sensed the pain he had experienced was nothing compared to what was to come. He looked through the lockup room grill door to see if anyone was waiting outside to rescue him. He hoped Comrade Kumaran had come to release him. He wished MLA Rajan would come to the rescue.

"Agree to what Jacob asks for. He will spare you if you leave the police custody with no scene. Or else… be like the dead girl floating in the stream." Neelan said nothing. The policeman who had the empty tumbler in his hand hurled it to the ground. It hit the floor and bounced off the wall, coming to a rest near Neelan's eyes. He looked to see if any drops of water was left in it. A third policeman walked into the room. Neelan looked up. It was a familiar face, Constable Bhaskaran Nair from his village. He stared blankly at Neelan for a long minute before walking out of the room. It seemed he didn't want to be a part of this.

Policemen continued their brutal interrogation, hoping to get Neelan to confess. They lifted and tied him to a tall wooden bench, with his hands and legs hanging down. A heavy wooden roller rolled over his thighs. The pain was almost unbearable and Neelan screamed in agony. A policeman shoved a piece of cloth into Neelan's mouth so no one outside could hear him. The monsters in khaki shirts and shorts took a break; they were afraid the frail man would die in their custody. After the policemen had done their worst, Neelan was not sure if he had all of his body parts on him. He couldn't feel anything except the massive heaviness in his head. A heavy head with veins cut off from the trunk. Like all his parts, scattered around the room. After a few hours, Sub-Inspector Jacob tied Neelan's feet together with a wire and lifted him up. Soon he hung upside down from a hook on the ceiling. He kicked Neelan to swing like a pendulum; a naked one hung from the ceiling. He pounded every inch of his body with a baton, without making any mark on him.

Once he was cut down, Neelan lay on the ground; his face stuck to the dirty cement floor stale with urine and drenched in savagery. At daybreak, he woke up from the harrowing dream; from the heavy boot steps closing in. His body was still shaking.

"You have a visitor. Get up."

Finally, Comrade is here to rescue me; I should tell him everything they did to me, he thought and struggled to get up; gathering all the strength he had. The policeman standing next to him helped him to rise, but he couldn't stand on his feet. His muscles and bones had melted away. A policeman pulled him up and made him sit on a chair outside the cell. Slowly he turned towards the open window where a man was sitting facing him.

Bright morning sunlight flooding into the room seared Neelan's vision, making everything blurry. He squinted his eyes to see if that would help him recognize who was in the room, not Comrade, not the MLA; it was not anyone he had ever seen. Scared, Neelan continued staring until he was able to see the person clearly. He didn't look scary, but Neelan didn't want to trust anyone anymore, even if it was someone he had always trusted. The last few hours had taught him to trust no one and fear everyone. The stranger was well dressed. A smile on his face displayed his eagerness to talk, and his eyes expressed compassion for the battered man. Neelan felt a bit relieved. The man introduced himself as Advocate Sivadasan, the public prosecutor, a lawyer appointed by the government to help people like him. He promised his interest was nothing but that of helping Neelan. Advocate Sivadasan explained his dilemma. There was no one ready to swear, in court, that Neelan was innocent. On the contrary, there are many to give false witness against him. His hopes faded when he learned that even his own people wouldn't be there for him. He cursed himself for failing to alleviate the fear of his own folks… even after breathing the breeze of freedom blown over them, even after hearing the sound of liberation that lifted them.

"Laws mean nothing if change doesn't happen within. It takes time. Invisible bondages cannot be erased that easily," the prosecutor emphasized the reality. He suggested that Neelan agree to a plea deal.

"It is only an interim adjustment," he said. Neelan knew what this meant. A game played again and again where an innocent is made to plead guilty and the one who did the crime becomes innocent. The prosecutor promised to bail out Neelan immediately by applying a loophole in the law, claiming his client's insanity. Neelan got a promise of short confinement, and an assurance of quick justice. "Why fight the mountain when we are feeble and a rolling stone can crush us?" Sivadasan convinced him that this was the best decision in a corrupt system.

"That is, indeed, a brilliant idea, Prosecutor. We will take care of him very well." Sub-Inspector who was listening to the conversation outside joined them, assuring all his support.

Neelan raised his head and looked at the Public Prosecutor. "You can trust me. I know the judge and the judge knows me well. We have helped so many people like you." Neelan looked away onto the opposite side. There was a life-sized picture of

Gandhi on the wall. Neelan stared at the Father of the Nation, whose image stared back at him with an innocent smile. The same way the government lawyer smiled at him was the same way Sub-Inspector Mathew Jacob smiled at him a moment ago. Neelan nodded in agreement.

To the judge, Neelan spoke just as he had been instructed by the prosecutor. He trusted in his advocate's advice, but the judge sentenced him to a life-term imprisonment. When Neelan was taken out of the court and led to the prison, he looked for the prosecutor. The man was nowhere to be found. Neelan knew, he was busy in the company of Sub-Inspector Mathew Jacob and C.L Rajan MLA counting the tainted money—the wage for selling Neelan's freedom and denying justice to Radha. Once again, they had reassured the world that the rich and powerful are always above the law.

When the new pro-labor government took over, many convicts were let off at the recommendation of the Jail Review Committee. Neelan was released at the end of his sixth year of incarceration. Neelan returned to his village, his shack had disappeared. In its place there stood a large treehouse with a concrete base. Muthalali built an elegant place… a place for the elite and the influential to congregate, to put a price on the freedom of their next victim. Homeless and nowhere to go, Neelan walked to the Junction that belonged to no one. There he had the freedom to sleep anywhere when everyone left. He called it his home and it had no doors for anyone to close. It had no roof, but it was safe for him. He let his past go by, and his heart became lighter and lighter. When it became empty, music began to fill his home and everyone became part of him.

~

NEELAN WAS A living image from Nila's adolescent years that never got erased. Neither she nor any of her friends from childhood know who he really was or cared to find out his past. What really influenced them was the song he filled the air they breathed with, those melodies that got trapped in their brain folds. It made them nostalgic and, in a split second, they could go back to that time. That is why Nila had her flute packed among her other belongings when she moved to America. She let it sit on the apartment's windowsill. Some days when she felt lonely, she would crank open the window a tiny bit for the reed to breathe. Then she would sit before God Krishna's statue with her eyes closed. In the peak of the ecstasy of her devotion, she began to hear songs heard thousands of years ago by those *Gopikas*, the girls who danced around God Krishna. ...and soon she would transcend to one among them and danced to the tunes that filled her heart.

At the farmer's market, I met a woman with the gift to see the past.
Really???

i
Some questions never find answers
They wait and wait
Like the mind of the deep ocean
Its eyes wide open even in deep sleep
Hoping the waves would cease
Hawkeyed storms hover in circles chewing its heart
Still, it waits and waits

ii
Some things we always want to say
But we are unable
Fear splutters through muffled words
Unspoken mind, unheeded cry
Sprawling tree with its leaves drooping
Its shallow grooves and veins nesting memories
Its shade soaked in tears

Farmer's Market

URING THE SUMMER months, Nila made it a point to visit, whenever possible, the Minneapolis farmer's market on Saturday mornings. She entertained no other plans during this time, even if it was inconvenient for Ashok to join her. The smell of garden-fresh vegetables and herbs that floated in the crisp morning air always refreshed her mind and soul. It also spurred nostalgic moments for her, like the feel of walking under the snake gourd and bitter melon pergolas at her ancestral farm in Kerala. She loved to float among the smiling faces in the market like a butterfly, enjoying the buckwheat honey sticks that she always bought in bunches as soon as she got there. Looking at the creativity displayed by vendors arranging the colorful vegetables, stirred her imagination. Inherently, she was drawn to the brightly colored freshly cut flowers, inhaling them and occasionally feeling their petals when the vendor was distracted. For her, the farmer's market was not just a place to buy fresh vegetables, she felt she blended in well with the crowd and felt she really belonged. It always enveloped her in an extremely delightful way.

The crowd never failed to display its array of hues and flavors and Nila fit in with ease every time she was there. Its cultural symphony made her feel like a piece of a giant collage where everyone came together, shattering the walls separating their minds.

One such beautiful Saturday morning, on Memorial Day weekend, Nila and Ashok took to the road for their Saturday ritual. By the time Ashok and Nila found a parking space and arrived at the market, it was past ten o'clock. Nila breathed in the energy that filled the air. She couldn't avoid looking at the families, enjoying hot-dogs and munching on corn on the cob at the vendor's booths parked at the entrance. The farmer's market and the adjacent Annex, which sold everything from clothes to handmade jewelry, were way busier than usual. She paused for a moment wanting to buy the irresistible pickles immersed in vinegar, but then she decided to get them on her way out.

Vendors stacked plenty of herbs, spinach, kale, and almost all varieties of squash and peppers, but as always, she had no luck finding her favorite string beans. It took her more than two hours to do most of her shopping on that overcrowded day. She was very dissatisfied with her buying experience and felt her bargaining skills hadn't worked that day. Almost all the vendors were not in any mood to shrink their prices. They knew the mounting crowd would eventually swallow their inventory before the market closed.

It was almost noon and Ashok was losing patience. He asked her to hurry up as both of them had their hands full of vegetable bags. She agreed to go home, but before she turned to go back home, she did a 360-pan view of the market to see if she had missed anything. Immediately, she left all her bags at Ashok's feet and briskly paced between the jewelry stalls to the other side. Ashok shook his head in frustration. He had no choice but to wait in the sun with a bunch of vegetable bags scattered around him.

Nila stopped at a vegetable stall run by an elderly Hmong woman who wore a traditional head wrap with a flannelled red scarf. Though tired looking, she held a mysterious smile on her wrinkled face. The vegetables she sold looked surprisingly fresher than the ones other vendors had on display. Nila didn't remember visiting her stall earlier. She thought the woman might have brought freshly picked harvest from the farm in the last hour and that was why she hadn't seen her. Nila picked up a few bundles of string beans that smelled fresh and asked, "How much if I buy four bundles?"

"Ten dollars, dear," the lady replied with genuine fondness.

"Can you give me one more bundle for the same price?" Nila bargained with her, but she didn't have a lot of faith. It always felt good for her even if she bought something a penny lower than its marked price.

Vegetable lady's eyes lit up more than before, and she looked into Nila's eyes for a moment and laughed. She answered with a sweetened voice but with little hesitation, "Of course, my child, if you insist. I would even give you all of these for free if I could. You look very familiar to me. Maybe... I know you."

"What? What did you say, Ma'am?"

"I know you... I know you," the lady said with a grin while she bagged the string beans.

"You must be mistaken ... I haven't seen you before," Nila said with a smirk as vegetable woman while grabbed the twenty dollar bill Nila gave her.

"I am glad you came to me, dear."

"Why?" Nila asked while she grabbed the change and the bag from the woman.

"Don't you remember... you were going to be drowned in a bus accident? You missed the bus. But your friend got on and sat on the seat that should have been yours." She paused and continued in an impeccable voice. "You can control your journey. How can you change your destiny?"

Nila froze, for how long she didn't know. When her mind began to work, she turned and darted toward her car. On her way, she didn't see Ashok or the pickle seller or the pickle jar that she had craved when she had first got to the market

Ashok screamed, "Nila... Stop!" but she didn't hear him. He scrambled to grab all the stuff and ran behind her, sensing something had gone wrong.

Even after reaching home, Nila was unable to recover from the unsettling incident at the market. Her mind raced with so many questions.

"A Hmong woman, born in some other corner of the world, who I've just met today, knows me and my life. How...? How could she know my past?"

Ashok was also taken aback by this, but he struggled to come up with something that would convince her.

"It is strange, dear; I've heard some people can read minds. Some can predict the future. Let it go, don't let it bother you." He continued with some humor to ease her. "Maybe you bargained too much, and she wanted to mess with your mind."

"It was Fatima, my friend who died. Did she die because I didn't take the bus that morning?" Nila broke into tears. Nila sensed that Ashok was losing his temper, but she let him calm her down.

"You're overthinking. Fate... who has control over it? There is nothing you could have done, period."

All that day and evening Nila felt miserable and gloomy. She wanted to take a long nap to rid herself of the heaviness that was settling in her mind. But she couldn't sleep. Thoughts of Fatima and everything that lead to her death overwhelmed her. She felt like a lone child who had lost her way in a fast-approaching monsoon storm.

~∘

Nila had lived with her maternal grandparents and her uncle's family in *Vedagiri* to attend college. Her uncle Krishnan was the regional manager for a company that produced infant milk products. He was overseeing the whole of South India, which involved much traveling and he was rarely home. This made Aunt Sarada, his wife, frustrated and overassertive with her children. She complained that the grandparents pampered them too much, that their behavior was getting out of control. Maloo, her cousin, was a ten-year-old playful girl with lots of energy. She was thrilled when she learned Nila was joining them for a few years. She knew that having a *Chechi*, an older sister to explore the world with her, whom everyone trusted, would gain her more freedom and immunity from Amma's restrictions. She called her Nilechy, combining 'Nila' and 'Chechy,' for big sister.

Her brother, Ravi, was a seven-year-old prince, ruling his own territory around the home. He hated wearing anything other than tiny trousers on his frail body. With his long curly hair hanging past his shoulders and walking barefooted, he earned the nickname *Mougli* among the village kids. He spent most of his time after school roaming around in the yard, chasing dragonflies and butterflies. A few months before, he had built a tree house in the almond tree next to the kitchen, which was also a hiding place among the banana plants covered in dry leaves. He was always prepared to face an invasion from the neighboring enemy kings, or the dinosaurs that could escape from Jurassic Park at any moment. Two rabbits he petted kept him amused and hated anyone else tending them. The rabbit house was built onto the retaining wall that separated the tiny hill that grew tapioca plants. Nila was amazed at his construction skills when her cousin Maloo said Ravi didn't accept anyone's help to build the house made with dirt and bricks. She thought it was a piece of artistic excellence for a child of his age. It looked like a tiny temple built with wooden frames in front and a tiny trussed roof with roof tiles laid over them.

For Nila, *Vedagiri* was always a place of mystery from her childhood. Her mother had told her about the history surrounding the region and it had developed a curiosity in her. But she suppressed her interests when grandma warned her, the very day she arrived, against joining Maloo in exploring the hill. She explained it wasn't safe for kids due to snakes and wild animals roaming around.

The place had gotten its name from Veda-Vyasa, the author of Hindu Epic *Mahabharata*. It is believed he had an ashram, a sacred residence at the peak of the Vedagiri hill located in the middle of the village. Remnants of the monastery can be seen at the top of Vedagiri hill even now. It is believed that the *Pandavas*, the five princes from the Mahabharata epic, visited Veda-Vyasa during their exile life. What made Nila really wonder was when she learned about the pond at the top of the hill that never went dry. Even during the hottest summer, when every well in the village dried up, the pond had water from the springs.

Nila would take the bus to college which was almost forty-five minutes from home. She always arrived a few minutes early so she could have a quick visit to the Devi Temple which was next to her bus stop. The Temple and the adjacent market was where the villagers came to breathe and vent their frustrations and emotions. During the day, rice fields and nearby textile mills kept the local men busy. The remaining ones loitered and gossiped sitting in the Bhagavathi's tea shop (Teashop of Goddess), where the proprietor, Narayanan, sat behind the tall glass case which was full of deep-fried split bananas dipped in batter, *bondas,* and steamed rice cakes. By around four 'o clock in the afternoon, the temple area would get busy with devotees and snack vendors. By then a few young men would have sat on the culvert stones that were over the tiny creek. It separated temple property from the market. They teased the girls who passed by, but would become cautious when any approaching police jeeps appeared and would even disappear from sight momentarily if they suspected a police officer was around. When Isaac Mathew was in charge as the Sub-Inspector of Police at *Ettumanoor* police station, a bunch of policemen came around wearing civilian dress and booked them all for teasing and harassing young women. They had to stay in the police lockup overnight in their underwear and were released only after their parents came to bail them out.

In the evening, there was always a patient crowd waiting for their turns to grab hot, salted peanuts in a cone from the boy who sold them. Their smell and taste was addictive. The young boy's four-wheeled cart was equipped with a kerosene stove to roast the peanuts. Skillfully, he sieved out sizzling peanuts from the burning sand that had turned into charcoal dust. Next to him, a few feet away, there was a woman selling vegetables. She had a large red dot on her forehead. She never stopped chewing betel leaf with areca nut and tobacco making her lips permanently blood red. No one dared to ask her name or whereabouts. She appeared there a few years ago, after a devastating monsoon storm that lasted for few days. After that, she was the only one selling vegetables in the village. The woman sat facing the temple, and from there she could see the deity of the temple, Goddess *Durga*. Many street vendors tried every trick to get the coveted spot she had. They tried to chase the woman away but were not successful. What was really strange was, a few others opened vegetable shops after she arrived and no one could make it work. Either there would be some mishap or obstruction before they could begin the business. The last one who attempted to open a business was a Muslim man from the neighboring town of Athirampuzha; he came with gunny bags full of vegetables. When he opened the first bag, a cobra hissed and jumped out, and the poor man ran for his life. After that incident, no one attempted to compete with her.

Rumors quickly spread everywhere. Some said the woman was possessed or was Devi herself, to watch and protect the villagers. They reasoned this because they lived in a land that was holy and blessed through Sage *Parusu Raman,* an incarnation of Lord *Maha Vishnu,* and later by the presence of Veda-Vyasa. The woman sold vegetables from dawn and was the last one to leave in the evening. Once every few weeks, she would disappear for few days. During that time, the villagers would buy their vegetables from a nearby town or manage with the greens from their own backyard. After she returned, her face had an extra glow that lasted for few days, and the red dot on her forehead blazed in the sun. During that time, no one looked into her eyes for they feared the fire in them would eventually blind them.

Maloo claimed she had talked to the vegetable lady several times and found nothing odd about her. Moreover, she had felt the lady was especially nice to her. Each time she gave Maloo a couple of tender okra without Maloo even asking and she had never told the woman about her liking for them. She thought it was just a coincidence. But Nila was certain the woman was strange and took the warning from her grandmother seriously. Grandmother had advised Nila to stay away from her as she thought the woman was shrouded in mystery. *Better to stay safe than feel sorry later,* she thought. Nila never ventured to go near her, but she always spied on her while she waited for the bus. That didn't last long, though. One day while she threw a quick glance at her, the woman also looked at her at the same instant. From that distance, Nila could see her bright wide eyes. At that moment, a sudden spark pierced inside her, engulfing every fiber of her body in heat. She quickly shut her eyes and stood still for a few minutes until she regained her poise. After that day, she always looked in the opposite direction, ignoring the woman's presence till the bus arrived.

As Nila's presence in her family home became comfortable, Maloo's aspirations for more increased. She always believed being in the company of her older cousin brought less scrutiny from her mom. Maloo wanted to take full advantage of the situation. Aunty Sarada and their grandparents trusted Nila and knew she would never make a bad decision or do anything that would get them both into trouble. So while Nila was busy with her classes and assignments, Maloo envisioned and masterminded potential opportunities to get out of the house and to maximize the possibilities of exploring everything she had always wanted to explore. Nila never wanted to go out of the house, even to her friend Fatima's house, without permission. She tried hard to convince and limit Maloo's unpredictable adventures to the vicinity of their property and the adjacent coconut groves. They made a swing by tying ropes on the hanging branch of the mango tree in the backyard. On sunny days, they walked through the rice fields, catching baby fishes from the water canals that separated each property in the farm. They gave all their catches to Ravi. He grew them in small glass jars and plastic bottles in the rabbit house, hoping they would enjoy each other's company.

It was the Pooja Holiday and the schools were closed. Maloo and Nila had kept their books as an offering at the feet of the statue of the Goddess *Saraswati*, the giver of wisdom and learning. This had become the most favorite holiday for school kids, as no one would ask them to study or do homework.

Maloo was looking forward to this day and wanted to take full advantage of the holiday. Their grandpa was the temple's festival committee chairman. The remaining adults in the family volunteered in the temple activities during auspicious days. She anticipated the last day when the adults would be back by late evening after the lengthy ceremonies and celebrations. She was certain they would leave them home as it was too tiring for her, and Ravi would join his Grandpa. He never missed any opportunity to hang out in the temple. The meticulous sculptures and carvings embedded in the temple's architecture amazed him every time and he never got tired of it. He was lost in the temple often and was almost always found engrossed in some piece of art, forgetting everything else. Elephants were his other fascination. He had made friends with every mahout who came to the temple and had a huge collection of rings made with the hair from pachyderm tails. He wore them on his fingers when something scared him, or when left alone at home.

~

MALOO CHARTED OUT and continued masterminding her exuberant plans. She didn't share with Nila for fear of how she would react. But she felt confident of coming up with an idea to convince Nila to partner in her defiant but exhilarating plans. That morning, she woke up early and waited anxiously for the adults to leave for the temple. Her mom noticed this and expressed her surprise.

"Why are you awake this early, Maloo? You never get up till the sun is over the roof when there is no school," Aunt Sarada asked.

"Oh… nothing, Mom, I forgot about the holiday," she replied on a whim, giving no clue to what was cooking in her head.

Everyone had left for the temple leaving just the two of them at home. Silence had gripped the whole house as if a thunderous storm had ended. Maloo had never experienced such calmness at home in her recent memory. She could even hear her own heartbeat. Nila was on the back veranda, ironing Grandpa's clothes.

Maloo couldn't wait anymore, she ran out through the front door. She climbed over the half wall that bordered the courtyard and scanned the road as far as she could in the direction of the temple. She couldn't recognize anyone as her mom and grandparents had already disappeared into the strangers. They had become part of the anonymous party.

"Yes! They are out of sight." She breathed a sigh of relief and ran to Nila liberating herself with the newfound freedom.

"Let's go climb the hill!" In excitement, Maloo forgot she needed to talk to Nila to make her buy into her idea. But she had to work fast because there was no better time than now to try out the adventures she'd planned. She was confident she could convince Nilechy to take a tiny risk for a lifelong memory.

"What? What did you say?" Nila screamed, arching her eyebrows in shock.

"Please… please, my dear sister," Maloo blubbered.

"No… We cannot go there without an adult with us. The whole village is in the temple," Nila retorted.

"Nilechy, you are almost an adult. If we don't go today, we will never see the top of the hill. It is my dream." Maloo began to cry and hoped in her heart her tears would eventually change Nilechy's mind.

"Stop crying, Maloo. The whole village can hear you."

"Nilechy, you hate me. That is why you never listen to me."

Nila didn't know if she should laugh at Maloo's silly tantrum or ignore her, but in any case, she wanted Maloo to stop crying. Nila paused for a moment while Maloo continued to whine.

She responded, "Well… we will do one thing, let's go to Rema Teacher's home that is on the way. We will ask my friend, Fatima, to join us. The teacher will take care of her little boy."

A victorious smile sprung in Maloo's face, but her tears didn't stop flowing down her cheeks. She didn't bother to wipe them away as she didn't want to lose the sympathy she had worked hard to win from Nila.

It was not just because her friend Fatima lived with her,

visiting Rema Teacher's home always delighted Nila. She was a big admirer of the teacher. She experienced an inner peace in the presence of the down-to-earth woman she'd never felt with anyone else. In the last few years, the teacher had become very popular throughout Kerala for getting involved in social issues and community uplifting programs. When the *Sastra Sahitya Parishad*, a movement to promote the growth of scientific outlook among common people started, she played a major role in the success of its key initiatives. When the mass movement to tackle illiteracy was at its peak in India, the teacher motivated others to attract volunteers from every walk of life. Nila still remembered the day, watching the government-run TV *Doordarshan,* the only TV channel that was available, saying that Kerala was now fully literate. Aisha, a sixty-eight-year-old grandmother, an illiterate who had gone through the program, was filmed reading from the Koran on a stage with the then prime minister, VP Singh.

Later, Teacher rose to fame to become the voice of abused and exploited girls. She had gotten involved in the notorious sham marriage called *Arabi Kalyanam* involving an orphan Muslim girl named Fatima. The illicit practice of young girls getting married to older men who had arrived from the Arab countries for short visits, targeting the poverty-stricken families in the Malabar region of Kerala.

Local Islamic clerics solemnized the weddings with the silent approval of local politicians who had vested interests. Many of these marriages were short-lived from a few days to months, ending through triple ta-laq, a religiously accepted form of divorce, where the husband's threefold repetition of the word 'Talaq' absolves the marriage. Always, the broker walked away with a commission, leaving the girls with uncertainty and a shattered life that could never be mended.

FATIMA HAD LIVED in an orphanage since the age of five, when her mother had died in an accident at a construction site where she was a laborer. She had no memory of her father who had abandoned the family soon after her birth. A few days after she turned sixteen, the orphanage authorities forced her into wedlock with a fifty-two-year-old Saudi Arabian native man against her wishes. They threatened the girl and mentally tortured her till she agreed to the marriage. Two months into the marriage, the man in a flowing, white robe with red and white checked head-gear just disappeared, leaving Fatima with the seed of inhibition that would chain her existence in the society. The orphanage hesitated to take the pregnant girl back and she had nowhere else to go. Late that evening, she jumped into the nearby river from the bridge, to free herself from all the worries. But she couldn't find solace in that attempt; fishermen who witnessed her jump saved her before she drowned. She pleaded with the local police officer to keep her in lockup. She thought it would be safer for her than wandering the streets or sleeping in the bus shelter for the night. Her story was immediately reported to the media, and it soon found its place among the national headlines. The entire state hung its head in embarrassment by the resurfaced stain of the past that everyone thought was buried. There was a public outcry. The human-rights organizations urged the government to take action.

Rema Teacher had never married and was a well-respected teacher at the local high school. While the women's organizations worked with women's shelters for Fatima's rehabilitation, the teacher walked into the police station to visit the girl. She looked into the morbid eyes of Fatima, and after few moments they both couldn't control their emotions. Fatima fell into the teacher's arms.

Wiping her tears, teacher said, "You are the daughter I always wanted. I am here for you as long as you need me."

Holding her hand, she took Fatima home. At that moment,

even the callous Kerala State policemen felt a jolt in their hearts, but unrevealing their feelings they watched the culmination of benevolence and susceptibility at its purest state. Standing still outside, the public and reporters watched them leave. On that day the teacher won the trust of the people, and in their hearts, they raised her as the defender of social justice, a voice for the voiceless. Teacher demanded a strong legislation be made to enforce laws that curbed exploitation of children and closely monitored communities and orphanages where children were vulnerable. Teacher's fervent efforts didn't go smoothly. She had many death threats from the cohorts of the corrupt who used religion for their gains. She charged like a stallion and continued the fight unheeding to pressures, championing the causes that mattered to her most. For Fatima, she never had to worry about her future or her son, Najeeb.

NILA MET FATIMA for the first time at the bus stop, where they both boarded the bus together to college and they were immediately thick friends. Fatima was working on her master's degree to become a social worker. She dreamed of working with young girls growing up in challenging circumstances.

NILA WAS DRAWN out of her revelry when they heard the announcement through the temple's loudspeaker about the commencement of programs. Maloo signaled, and they both ran in opposite directions. They made sure the front door, and the kitchen door that faced the backyard, and the paddy field were locked from the inside. They then assembled near the dining room window where they carefully removed its two metal grates, one by one jerking it upwards and pulling it down at an angle. A secret within the household, to get into the house if doors were locked, and one didn't have the key on them. One by one they slipped out and placed the bars back in place.

Teacher's house was halfway between their home and the *Vedagiri* hill. To elude attention, they decided to avoid the main road. They walked toward the backyard, then in haste cut across the rice field that no one was working that day. Farmers were between crops waiting for the northeast monsoon rains. The village hadn't gotten much rain in the past few months and it made the land extremely dry and cracked. From where they stood, the entire farm looked like a large spider web. Maloo held on to Nila's hand while they raced to avoid getting their feet stuck in the cracks.

When they reached the alley going toward Teacher's backyard, they took a break and sat on either side of the wooden base where the giant water wheel was mounted. The shade of a hanging branch from the large mango tree that stood at the edge of teacher's property gave them a little relief from the scorching sun. Restless, Maloo climbed over the bamboo stand from where Cheruman treaded the wheel leafs. He pushed the water up to the field from the canal that was flowing in the opposite direction. Though her feet didn't reach the wheel, she sat on the crossbar and mimicked Cheruman's famous song:

> *KaruthaPenne... Karutha Penne ...*
> *Neelakashathintethamaraknanne...*
> *entechankukavarnnorusundari penne*
> *thazhottuthazhottu nee varumbo*
> *entheninakkithrachanthm-azhake...*

Oh, dark girl… Oh, dark girl
Entrancing eye of the blue sky
Oh stunning, you stole my heart
Why are you so charming when you come down?
Why do you laugh so loud before you reach me?
Come down… come down, my sweetheart
I will make you my wife; I will take you to the ocean

Oh, dark girl Oh, dark girl
Once I was so handsome
Jealous sun burned me to charcoal
Can you fall over me and I will turn into a prince?
Shall I ask the east wind to bring you to me?
Come down… come down my sweetheart
I will make you my wife; I will take you to the ocean

Cheruman, who was profoundly deaf, would sing the song louder and louder while thrashing the wheel leaves with all his might. He was heard from far away on quiet afternoons, wherever the wind carried his voice. His pacifying voice hallowed the village's soul. Birds and farm animals craned their head in his direction. It was not an exaggeration, even the senseless water buffaloes plowing the paddy fields held their breath to listen to him. During the summer evenings, with delight, villagers watched him fly over the wheel. He was faster than yarn fiber being spit out through the spinning machines at the nearby textile mill. His black, skinny, muscular body, almost naked except for a tiny, muddy loincloth around his waist, hung like a giant bat on the large bamboo poles erected on either side. He never rested and was seen till the large orange sun disappeared into the tree lines behind him, making him a shadow that blended into the night.

Nila and Maloo entered Teacher's home through the backyard,

then walked toward the front of the house through the nutmeg trees. The trees in the yard were dusty and were in need of a good shower to tidy them up, but it still felt much cooler and serene walking by them. Fatima was sitting on the porch floor reading a story to her five-year-old son Najeeb. They were both totally engaged in the story, unaware of the guests standing outside. Signaling Maloo to be quiet, Nila tiptoed toward the half wall around the porch. Maloo cautiously followed. They listened to Fatima read the story from *Panchatantra*, the ancient collection of fables. It was the story of a herd of elephants looking for water. They passed through a deserted city, populated only by mice. The mice, afraid of being trampled by the large herd, requested the elephants take a different path, a request their leader graciously agreed to. Years later, the mice heard of the elephants being captured by the king's army hunters. They rushed to help the elephants. They gnawed at the ropes which tied the elephants and set them free.

"A friend in need is a friend indeed, Najeeb." On hearing those words, Fatima raised her head and looked sideways. She was totally surprised.

"You guys! Come on in. Why didn't you call me earlier?" she complained.

"We were just enjoying your story. Fatima, you are a beautiful storyteller," Nila teased. They all burst into laughter for the joy in unexpectedly being with each other.

The teacher was not there, though. She had gone to Kottayam to visit some of her volunteers. There she was planning the details of a campaign against child labor and their exploitation among the restaurants and textile retailers. She was skeptical of the campaign's success. They were anticipating resistance from the powerful industries and expected very little support from the media who wouldn't risk their advertisement revenue from the alleged industries.

Maloo felt uneasy and disappointed, for there was now a risk that their plan could be dropped unless Teacher returned quickly. She knew it was impossible for Fatima to leave her son home alone to join them. Seeing Maloo's sudden sad face, Nila tried to make her feel better by rubbing her back. She put her hand over her shoulder like chums in her long-ago grade school. "Let's continue." Truly it was not just because she didn't want to disappoint Maloo, but she was way more excited to explore the hills that were a mystery to her ever since she heard of them.

"We stopped for a quick visit. We had some time before we go to the temple." Without further delaying their plans, Nila bid goodbye without any mention of their current pursuit.

From Teacher's home, they quickly crossed the Anamala road to take the narrow mud road that bordered the cattle feed plant and the hill. It was quiet and still there with no one to be seen in the vicinity due to the holiday. The stale air from the factory exhaust was trapped below the hill, and the wind had not found its way under the hill to carry away the stench of old coconut oil cakes. They ran as fast as they could to pass it. When they reached the turn to climb the hill, they paused to take a deeper breath.

"From here the hill doesn't look that steep," upbeat Maloo said to assure her un-waning energy in her pursuit. It was hot and the sun was almost above them. Their shadows made them look like two dwarfs climbing the hill for the Golden Nugget placed on the top. As they ascended the hill, they stomped their plastic sandals to scare any snakes away which might be hiding under the dry leaves on the ground. On their way up, they stopped at a collection of huge standing rocks that represented characters from the *Maha Bharatha* story. Adjacent to them, there was a flat stone that had feet of the sage Veda-Vyasa carved on it.

"He had large feet," Maloo chuckled, placing her feet over the footprint.

"Maybe people who lived thousands of years ago were way bigger than we are. They were giants who could even fight with wild animals and lift huge stones like this." And with that, Nila placed her foot in the footprint, cheered in the excitement and continued climbing.

When they reached the top of the hill, astonishment made them forget their exhaustion. They felt like they were on the top of the world. The sky was clear and small clouds floated over them, casting shadows over the residents. A pleasant breeze welcomed them, making the scorching sun much more amiable.

"We rule the world!" Maloo screamed as she raced to climb to the top of a rock that was at the peak of the hill. Nila followed her and pushed harder to reach the top before Maloo. After reaching the top, Nila raised her hands and let the breeze blow over her and the hill like an eagle and prayed, "Oh God, turn me into a bird that glides in the air, free with no worries." They held each other and looked toward the western horizon.

"That looks like the edge of the Arabian Sea," Nila said, pointing to a white line drawn between Earth and Heaven across the eastern horizon. Alappuzha, known as the Venice of the East, stood wrapped in green, like a lovely bride under the silver sky. *Vembanad Lake,* carrying the world's tastiest fish, pearl-spot, looked like a puddle of water with its bluish tint in the midst of green rice fields, separating Kottayam and Alleppey. Maloo took a twirl and screamed,

"Look!" She pointed in the opposite direction.

Nila, without losing her balance, turned back quickly, "Oh, my God. I don't believe this. Is that Western Ghats?" Nila exclaimed in disbelief.

They stood still, looking at the mesmerizing skyline of mountain ranges that bordered Kerala with the neighboring state of Tamil Nadu. In the bright, cloudless day, it was breathtaking for them to watch the shiny silver hills. Shadows of the rolling mountains' layers and the misty sky above it looked like the shadow of heaven cast over the horizon.

"No wonder Sages and the Goddesses hung around here." Expressing her joy, Nila made a full circle to see the panoramic view of the entire landscape. She held on to Maloo to avoid losing her balance over the rock.

Nila wished she could come early in the morning and watch the sunrise of this dream-like canvas. She was sure the sunset would be breathtaking, with the sun looking way bigger than what she saw on the rice field. She was certain there must be something strange about this place that kept everyone away. Even Uncle Krishnan ignored it whenever the hill came up in their conversations. He never missed any occasion to encourage them to fall into the lap of Mother Nature or to take time to bond with children between his hectic schedules. In fact, he was the one who took them to the dike at the edge of the lake that prevented the salt water from the ocean entering the freshwaters of Vembanad Lake. That day he took them to a toddy shop on a tiny island in the lake. There, they ate their stomach full of fried frog legs and fresh lake fish caught and fried in front of them. That visit was one of the best-kept secrets between those three, since toddy shops sold alcoholic palm wine that was forbidden for children.

Standing on top of the hill, they tried to guess the location of *Munnar hills* with its slopes covered in tea leaves, and the rolling meadows of *Wagamon hills.* They had visited both when they visited two summers ago when Nila's family came to visit her grandparents in Vedagiri. From there, they ran toward the pond that was protected with a two-foot high wall made with cut laterite bricks cemented in lime mortar. It seemed to be a recent addition, and its rusty-red color, and the dry moss over it, was a misfit for the unblemished landscape. The grass around the pond was lush and thicker with tiny yellow flowers decorating the pond area.

They couldn't stop laughing at the weirdness of the artwork of someone who had painted 'Anu+Rajive' on the wall in a heart symbol with whitewash. A large arrow pierced through the middle of the heart. Maybe the lovers wanted to profess their love to the whole world or was it the work of a cupid who wanted to make a pun at some Anu and Rajive's expense?

"So, this is the holy pond everyone talks about?" Maloo was not at all impressed by the size of the pond.

"What did you expect, Maloo? This is on the top of the hill probably one of the highest points in the plane. There are five springs that keep this from drying up. Don't you think it's a wonder? It still has water on a hot day like today, and never dries up even during the peak summer months."

Maloo didn't say anything. But she sat on the wall and quickly raised her feet and jumped towards the pond's edge. She looked at her reflection and sat next to the water. "It's oily." She quickly poked her finger in the water. "But cold."

"Don't play with that water, Maloo. It must be so old and we may want to keep the sanctity of the place," Nila advised. Maloo came out of the pond, and they walked toward the tree that stood between the pond and the old temple. The ground was covered with touch-me-not plants. With their feet passing over them, plants humbled themselves by folding their leaves. Nila sometimes called Maloo a 'touch-me-not' because she was very sensitive if someone didn't listen or pay attention to her. They walked carefully like the balancing skill game they played in the yard, where they walked barefoot as close to the plants as possible without disturbing them. If by chance one lost their balance, they would stamp on the plant, hurting themselves with the spikes on its stem.

As they approached the tree that blocked the view of the other side, remnants and part of the ancient temple began to emerge. Rocks surrounded the temple. On a raised mud platform, there stood huge granite stones that resembled deformed human giants. Someone had marked red stripes over the stones as if some religious rituals had been performed over them recently. In front of the temple, there were heavy stones placed on either side of the steps. *How could these stones be rolled up over this hill? And thousands of years ago! It is impossible for humans. Not even Bhima, the strongest of the five Pandava princes from Mahabharata epic could have done this.* Nila couldn't reason or disagree with the legend that said the stones appeared on the hill mysteriously after *Pandavas* completed their exile time.

Sitting on the flat stone by the temple, they talked about coming back to the place again, maybe with Teacher and Fatima. They thought Rema Teacher would know more stories and the history of the place. A cool breeze from the west swept through the place giving them goosebumps on a hot muggy day.

"I love this. How did this cold breeze get here on this hot day?" Nila feeling too cold held Maloo closer to give her a bit of warmth.

It seemed that the wind took all the life out of the trees, the air felt lighter and frigid. The whole place dropped into a dismal silence. Nila felt something weird was happening. Soon she heard a footstep slowly approaching from behind. Nila's heart stopped and she couldn't breathe. Maloo was shivering like a tuning fork, and Nila feared her drumming heart would explode in her tight arm.

No one ever told… could it be some wild animal? Wolf… Tiger? Oh my God… Oh, my God, she wanted to scream, but she couldn't. She had lost her voice and the strength to move.

The steps came closer, but then she caught the jingles of

anklets following the steps. Those steps faded into the ring of the jingles and became louder and louder, pushing everything in the universe as it came closer.

Though all her courage and cognition to act drained away, somehow, with the soothing resonance of the anklets, Nila found strength and some life sprouted within her. She quickly looked back to the temple area where she heard the sound.

"You..." Nila couldn't comprehend. She stood shaking and wanting to connect the face to the one she had seen somewhere before.

"Oh... it's the vegetable lady from near the temple!" Maloo yelled, becoming herself, and continued, "You sell the best okra in the world."

The women didn't say a word, but the elusive smile on her face didn't diminish.

"Oh... yeah!" Nila's fear subdued and she regained her composure. Even though Nila had seen her almost every day at the bus stop, it didn't occur to her it was the vegetable seller until Maloo realized it.

Her face was brighter than ever, her eyes wider than real life. In the bright sun, she was glistening with grace. The red line over her forehead resembled the one on the giant stone in the temple. Nila had never noticed the golden nose ring on her, but thought it was way larger than anyone wore. The stones on it sparkled to add an aura to her face. With her hair untied and loosely flowing, she resembled the goddess idol in the temple in town. Nila seriously wondered if she was truly possessed, as Grandma had said. Or if she was a crazy woman hanging around in these remnants of myths and fear, then coming down the hill to sell vegetables to make her living.

Nila badly wanted to escape from this self-created messy situation. She took a step back, grabbed Maloo's hand and quickly turned back. She walked as fast as she could toward the direction they'd climbed the hill. When they reached the tree that was between the temple and the pond, the women yelled, "WAIT!" Maybe it could be the fear that besieged them, or the spell of the woman, but they couldn't move another step… It was like their feet had been caught up in some kind of a trap. Nila turned back to listen to her, but the sun was right in her eyes. Shielding her eyes with her palm, she stared at the floor of the temple that was brighter than the glare of the blistering sun.

"It is not your curious mind, but the unchangeable fate engraved into your heart that brought you here. You can control your journey; how can you change your destiny?"

Vegetable seller! How could she be this silly? I hope this is a dream. Nila's mind boggled with a thousand questions. The lady continued, "Monsoon will arrive swirling and shoving with northeast winds with its accomplice, shaking the western mountains and the forests on its way. You will hear the hum of its messenger while you climb down. Don't let it wash you down. Don't let your eyes see daylight till its vengeance passes by. She kept repeating, "Let them not shed tears for you… Let them not shed tears for you." The sky turned dark over the mountains, and the wind gained strength while she spoke. They ran with all their might to escape from the woman and the fast-approaching storm. While going down the hill, they could still hear her roaring laughter over the rise and fall of the northeast wind and the squeal and flapping of the migratory birds that scrambled to regroup to escape to the Himalayas.

No one had predicted an early arrival of a violent *Thula Varsham,* the north-east monsoon breaking all the norms and etiquettes. Rainy season came in the Malayalam calendar month of *Thulom* which was always breathtaking but rarely caused disasters.

That night, the temple's steeple above the goddess idol toppled to the ground failing to withstand the wind. It rained all night. The dry land gulped as much as it could, but still, it flooded most low-lying areas in the village. A large branch of the Banyan tree that gave shade to the temple devotees for several centuries fell over the stores that operated under it.

"It is a very bad omen. Adversities will follow us until we please the Deity." *Thanthri*, the temple priest, reminded everyone who gathered to check the damages to the temple. Three months ago, a *Deva prashnam*, an astrological examination of the likes and dislikes of the goddess of the temple regarding the renovation of the temple was conducted. Then, astrologers and the priest foresaw and warned of devastations to the temple and the villagers if the renovations were not done immediately. Planning and fundraising had begun but was dragging for lack of interest from the locals.

When Nila woke up and walked into the kitchen for coffee, Aunty Sarada had already packed her lunch.

"The temple had some major damage after last night's storm," Auntie passed the message that Gopal told when he brought milk.

"Oh… it rained! So… is the milk way more watery than usual?" Nila was concerned about the fate of the temple, but still wanted to shove the worries aside and wanted to begin the day with some humor. They both chuckled and then burst into laughter when Auntie added, "Rain or shine, Gopal never adds water to the milk, he adds milk to it."

While sipping the *Brooke Bond* filtered coffee in her favorite hand-painted china cup, Nila came close to the kitchen window and looked at the sky. Clouds were thickening, without leaving even a tiny cleft for the morning sun to take a quick breath. The storm was brewing again after a momentary pause.

"Maloo has a fever; she is not going to school today. Did you guys go in the sun yesterday?"

Nila suspected inquisitiveness in Auntie's query and she ignored it by answering, "It looks like night. More rain seems on its way… let me get ready quickly and catch the bus before the rain hits." She hurried to her room.

Her bus to the college always started from the temple stop. It parked overnight there, after ending its last ride from the town in the evening. While she stepped out of the room, Maloo came running to her saying, "Chechi, did you forget what the lady said?" She reminded her of the previous day's incident on the hill. Nila was taken aback, but she shoved it away without showing her real feelings with a made-up laughter.

"Did you take that seriously? She is just a crazy woman." Nila downplayed her concern.

"See? It rained hard all night. The sun hasn't come out yet," Maloo groaned. While Nila caressed her hair and felt her fever, Maloo hugged her hard to change her decision. Then lightning struck and lit up the whole area. Before the jolting thunder was heard, the power failed. Immediately, like the stampede of wild horses over the roof, it rained for two hours.

Nila waited for the rain to be over and left home a few minutes early to catch the ten o'clock bus. By then the sky had cleared and the sun was up like nothing had happened. The road was filled with dirt, washed into it from the collapsed retaining walls from the nearby properties. Stone-paved narrow roads between them were totally wiped out. People were busy either removing the trees that had fallen over their homes or erecting temporary supports to hoist the fallen plantain trees.

As she approached the temple and bus stop area, she noticed the damage was much more severe there. A few of the houses had their roof tiles blown away, and a thatched house was totally flattened to the ground. She wondered if its residents were rescued or still underneath the debris.

It flooded the temple front and the creek, making the road a total mess. It was muddy and had puddles of water everywhere. She saw a big crowd gathered near the bus stop. There was a sense of panic. Some were moving aimlessly, not knowing where to go. Loud moans, loud cries, and whispers filled the area. She had no clue what had happened but she waited, a few yards away from them, for the bus to arrive. Out of curiosity, she glanced in the direction of the vegetable lady, but she was nowhere to be seen. She didn't know why or how it would matter to her; still, the lady's absence sparked a fear inside her.

Seeing Nila standing near the bus stop, Govindan Mama, her grandma's brother, came running toward her. "What a relief! We were worried you were on the bus!"

"What bus?" Nila rushed her words that went from shock to panic. He told her the seven o'clock bus that she usually took had lost control and fell into the river near the town. Two taxis full of people have gone to the accident location. All the telephone lines were broken and there wasn't much information. Then, in a subdued voice he said, "Five people died including the driver and many are at the medical college hospital..." He paused and hesitantly continued, "and... and... the Muslim girl who lives with Rema teacher in your college... was one among them."

"Fa... Fatima..." Nila evaporated into a vacuum. The whole world spun around her and she could see nothing but the woman on the hill. She was screaming at her, "Let them not shed tears for you... Let them not shed tears for you..." She held on to Govindan Mama. He slowly let her sit on the roadside.

∼

Ashok took an abrupt turn from Penn Avenue into the south gate of the apartment complex. He saw an open parking space which was his favorite spot under the vast black maple tree which cast its influence over the southeast corner of the parking lot. The tree had witnessed and helped them resolve almost all their discordances and squabbles, which they couldn't reconcile inside their home. He called it a 'Bodhi' tree, like the tree under which Lord Buddha was enlightened to find his path. Tree shade and freshness gave him a different perspective on his current state of mind, and he emerged with a positive stance.

After parking, he rolled down the windows and watched the lazy breeze lift a layer of Nila's hair caressing her forehead. He reclined his seat back and sat with his hands clasped behind his head for few moments. Then he tilted his face toward her to see if she was still disturbed. He thought for a moment, then slowly pulled his right hand and stretched it to rub her forearm.

"Cheer up, dear. There are too many things unknown to us in this world. We see the tip, then boast that we have seen everything. Our little minds reason on what we see... what we experience. It fools us and leads us to a mirage which is not even a shadow."

Then he asked her to breathe the fresh air and live in the moment thinking of nothing. He waited a few moments for her response and then added, "So, the lesson is… never again bargain with vegetable sellers."

"OK, dear!" she replied and soon their loud laughter spilled out through the car windows.

When they walked toward their apartment, Ashok looked back at the tree. A bright bar of sunlight filtering through the leaves fell over him, and the next moment it was gone, with a victorious smile he winked back at it.

Gone to India-fest at the state
capital
Ran into Thomas Thomas.
What a small world!

Blind eyes see only truth
Delusions never fool them
But we see mirages
Just what the mind wants us to see

We close our eyelids
Snubbing the light,
Dodging to alter fate.

We forget our future destined
Its details etched in undying fire
Fading lines on our palm hiding its traces.

Still, our thoughts bridge islands of desires
Looping through the lonely freeways
With day and night moving on its fast lanes
In the end, we reach nowhere but home.

Dr. Thomas Ape

I T WAS A Saturday in mid-August. The summer was still holding onto its warmth as Nila and her husband enjoyed the India Fest, which was held in conjunction with India's Independence Day on the Minnesota state capitol grounds. Nila loved this day and she would drag her husband Ashok and all their friends to attend the crowded festival and they would wander around as one big group. It reminded them of the festivities and celebration in India and made them feel at home.

The place was packed with several thousand people clad in ethnic attires from different regions of India. Many of the women flocked around henna artists and jewelry sellers. Booths displaying *sarees* and children's ethnic garments added color and a bazaar-like tone to the festivities. Kids formed long, winding lines at the face painting stations and at the front of arcade machines. Food vendors set up their stands toward the edge of the park to keep the hungry crowds from the main events. Occasionally a north wind swept through the area, replenishing the aroma of the spicy biryani that filled the fairground air with the sweet, sickly smell of funnel cakes, a smell carried from some county fair being held on the Mississippi River bank. Each time, the frivolous wind wanted to lift the canopies, sweeping away the paper plates and spilling the fountain drinks all over the place. Kitty-corner from where Nila sat, India's traditional dances were being performed under a pagoda that was erected for the event.

Sitting on a park bench under a large oak tree, Nila observed the whole area tucking into her favorite pistachio *kulfi* ice cream. While its chill slowly melted into the flavors of her childhood, she began to see everything and everyone through the eyes of a village girl that she had forgotten for a while. But she never let it leave her as that was truly who she was.

An affable crowd moved down through the steps from the capital building toward a small makeshift stand with both American and Indian flags flown on either side. The flags represented the inseparable identity of the people gathered there. Someone in the group signaled and shouted at the top of their lungs "The governor is here!" Nila craned her neck as far as it would go to catch her first glimpse of the high-ranking politician in person. He was the only one wearing a formal suit. It was a rich navy blue and he matched it with a brightly colored yellow tie. The people who gathered around him were in glossy, colorful knee-length *kurtas*. More people joined the governor while he strolled down. They wanted to meet the man they'd only ever seen on television. They shook the governor's hands, pleading with their friends to take a picture of them with the state's head. Like other politicians, he never showed any displeasure and displayed his pleasant smile and delight at being there.

Soon the official parade began with thousands of people in traditional finery walking by the flag station. Women in colorful *sarees* and girls in dazzling designs of long skirts and blouses gave an eyeful for the spectators. Men and women waved tiny Indian paper flags toward the governor who was the Chief Marshall for the parade. Each group featured cultural performances and mimicked the feats of street performers in India. Some wore giant costumes and walked on sticks. Kids danced along in costumes of Hindu gods and legends. Everyone was amused by the performance of a dancing Ganesh, the kid inside the elephant-faced god's costume. He had plenty of vigor and enthusiasm. While approaching the governor, he jumped up and down shaking the head so hard that the elephant's mask and the trunk fell apart into several pieces over the spectators, exposing his cute face. No one could stop laughing, and cheered for the boy as he moved forward, dancing as if nothing had happened.

It was after lunch when they all decided to visit different booths put up by different organizations that had a connection to the people of Indian heritage. That was when Nila ran into an old friend. Thomas Thomas (some used to call him Thomas Squared like Thomas²) her classmate from college. Nila immediately recognized the familiar face as she exited the Kerala Association's booth. Nila was in touch with all her classmates from college except Thomas. No one knew where he was and everyone was curious to find out his whereabouts because he was the odd one, the one whom no one thought would ever succeed in life. In total disbelief, she yelled, "Hey, Thomas Thomas! Is that you?"

After pausing for a moment in reminiscence and possibly because he was struggling to recognize Nila, Thomas' face lit up and he walked toward her.

"Hey Nila… what a pleasant surprise."

"Wow… this world indeed is small and round." And with that Nila turned toward Ashok and their friends who were few feet away. She introduced him boisterously.

"Look who is here. This is Thomas Thomas, my classmate from the Zoology Bachelor degree class in India." They all waved and mimed their pleasure in seeing him.

"Thomas Thomas," Ashok laughed whilst he said the two names.

"Has Nila lost her mind or is that really his name, Thomas

Thomas?" They reiterated his name, quietly looking at Nila in confusion. She repeated his name, when no one else did. They assumed she was simply accentuating his name.

"It has to be his name... why in the world would one have the same first and last name?"

"Doesn't it defeat the purpose of naming itself?" They chattered among themselves without Thomas hearing. They pondered the reasoning behind his naming. As the debate continued, Ashok joked, "Maybe his parents foresaw that one day he would leave India, and he would need to use his surname, which let's face it, would be too complicated for many to pronounce. So instead of embarrassing their son, with a difficult name, they gave him an easier name to use." The friends tittered at Ashok's insight, but he wasn't finished.

"Or maybe, since he is a Christian, maybe while he was being baptized, one of his relatives stammered and said his name twice. Not thinking anything of it, the priest entered it on the register twice, and it was never corrected." Everyone thought this extremely funny, even Thomas who cracked a smile even though it appeared he had been trying desperately not to. They continued teasing until Nila and Thomas joined in. Apart from the pun, they were all aware of how the naming practices in India worked. The majority of its inhabitants used the caste name as a surname amongst the upper casts. The caste system introduced through *Upanishads*, an ancient book of rules in Hinduism, was later enforced by the invading Aryans. They used it as a means to control and maintain their dominance over the dark-skinned native inhabitants. They used a caste to assign menial jobs and push them down, thereby, creating a society of classes and untouchables. Use of caste names reduced among higher caste levels after social reformation efforts. Many stopped using surnames that revealed their caste to avoid discrimination. Christians were obviously outside the caste boundaries and had no choice but to use their father's name or a family name that was derived on the peculiarity of the land where they lived. It kept changing as they moved from place to place. Their names were usually both biblical and inherited from grandparents, passed on from one generation to the next. In some cases, it could end up to be the same as it transpires from either side of a child's parents.

"None of us knew where you were. How did you end up here?" Excited, Nila couldn't wait to hear more about him after she left college.

"A few months ago, I joined the university here as an associate professor after completing my Ph.D. from Harvard University."

"Ph.D. from Harvard University. Wow!" Nila echoed at him in disbelief.

Thomas continued, "My dissertation was on the *resemblance of facial features, mannerisms, and behavior pattern amongst the native humans and primates*." When he said that they both looked eye to eye and Nila burst into laughter, controlling herself from screaming "Dr. Thomas Ape.'" She couldn't help herself, and they both laughed for a while leaving Ashok and his friends who were standing few feet away clueless. She thought he worked hard to legitimize the last name 'Ape,' given to ridicule him by their college classmates for him coming up with a silly theory of monkeys. 'Thomas Ape,' a name to connect him to Charles Darwin and the theory of evolution.

Unlike the past, she felt Thomas Thomas sounded very mature and wise in his conversation with the entire group. He was precise in his usage of words and weighed in with humor to suit the audience to captivate them. *Everyone in the group seemed fascinated by the wisdom and accomplishment of Professor Dr. Thomas Ape Ph.D.* Though she felt a bit jealous inside her heart, she felt happy that he had made a success of his life when he had always been the class clown. For a moment, she wondered how a trivial incident, that everyone had thought insignificant and had forgotten about, had become the inciting moment which fueled the passion inside him to become the success he was today.

Thomas Thomas's journey had begun in humiliation and ended in glory. By receiving his doctorate from Harvard University, and becoming the professor at a major university, he proved everyone else's prejudiced predictions wrong. To her, he was not just a person who had achieved his dream while following his passion, but he was someone who had found his purpose in life, which people search for but rarely find.

In college, Thomas was just a laughingstock and no one took him seriously. He thought of himself as naturally funny and wanted to bring humor to everything he did. In reality, he was a clown that had lost his wits. He had opinions and notions about anything and everything and had a tough time giving his tongue a rest. It was in the life science class, toward the end of the second year of college, when he came up with the monkey theory. Reviewing his annual research project, Father Varghese Mathew, a Carmelite priest and the professor of zoology, was devastated and furious over Thomas' report. In his research, Thomas came up with the theory that, the mannerisms, along with the facial features of monkeys, resembled that of native humans in each geographical region. What made the situation worse, and totally unforgiving, was the picture of the person he used for the Southern Indian region looked just like Fr. Varghese, except the monkey had more hair. Some mischievous ones in the class drew cartoons of the incident in the boy's restrooms and the college compound wall near the main gate. Their cartoons showed Father Varghese with a monkey face, and a tail coming out of his habit. The cartoon was signed by 'Thomas Ape, Son of Darwin.' From that incident, Thomas was forever known as 'Thomas Ape' within the campus. He was suspended for a month, but after that, life moved on and everyone thought normalcy had come back to his life. Mr. Ape was ignored as usual and he rolled into his own realm where he was often seen in the library buried in books.

Nila never saw or heard of Thomas again after college until this day. She was extremely happy to see him, but on the other hand, remembering his past brought up the hurt she had felt for him at the time. This was something she allowed herself to feel only when she was convinced Thomas was not trying to ridicule Father Varghese, rather he believed in his theory and was only wanting to make it convincing to everyone through the way he presented it. Though she'd had nothing to do with the whole ordeal, she considered apologizing to him on behalf of the whole class. But then decided to focus on the positive outcome rather than dig up the past. She always believed, good or bad, that everything happened for a reason, and it would eventually result in something better.

Nostalgia of childhood.
Village life circus and the visit
of Balan Mash as a holy man

Livid sky made beautiful rain drops
Gravid. Bearing the pain, holding breath
 Waning to emptiness
Letting its soul rain into destiny
Gobbling down its verve
 The hungry minds drown in it.
Meager ones cursed each other,
And, then drowned hungry
Orphaned dewdrops unnerved
Looked for a place to hide.
Shaking, leaves swept in the wind
Praying for the sun to come on its side
Raindrop the tear of the bygone
Seed for the impending,
Fruit of the existing
 Unable to cry, looked into itself
 Saw a new cloud forming within
 It's strengthening heartbeat kept erasing the past

SWAMI (The Holy Man)

T HE TIMING COULDN'T have been more perfect. Swami showed up in the village toward the end of the summer holidays. It was hardly a week after the traveling circus had left for their next gig. There was an emptiness felt by everyone when the entertaining gypsies and their tents disappeared from the landscape… a tint of gloom trapped in the air which waited for rain or something palliating to reset itself. The laid-back villagers had never enjoyed such an astounding treat in their life. Feats of dexterous acrobats and the gags of the absent-minded clown, kept them amused for a few weeks. Though the artists didn't speak the same language as the villagers, they still mingled with everyone like they were an element of their milieu. Everyone wanted the circus to stay forever. People gave them rice and coconuts along with access to their wells for water. Quickly the circus attracted people from near and faraway places. Families and children swamped the place in the evenings and weekends. Villagers felt important in their prominence and the local businesses thrived like never before. During the day, for a fee of one rupee, the circus people taught the children to ride unicycles and to walk on stilts. Nila had quit learning the unicycle after two falls, but she became an expert at walking tall on sticks. That year, Nila and all her friends walked on tall poles wearing costumes and large masks to entertain the crowd during the temple processions and village festivals. It was the same children who were playing in the rice field vacated by the circus company, who noticed Swami's arrival. He sat on a small stone at the edge of the hill that bordered the field. A small Neem tree made an umbrella over him, giving him shade during the hot hours. An ecstatic smile dwelled on his face permanently. He sat upright in deep meditation. His legs were crossed and his open palms rested on his knees facing the sky. He wore a loose, long orange robe covering his tall, slender body. His snow-like, long curly hair waved in the wind, and the uncombed gray beard reached his chest. His exposed skin looked like that of youth. The glow on his face rendered him a mystical look.

The news of the Holy Man's emergence spread all across the land quickly. By evening a big crowd had gathered around him. Reverently, in silence, they waited for him to open his eyes. Women and children offered petals and fruits at his feet, and bowed before him for his blessings, sitting in his vicinity. He ate nothing that was offered. He didn't even touch the fresh, tender coconut juice placed on a silver plate next to him. He didn't leave the place or open his eyes. Another day passed, but Swami still didn't open his eyes. The anxious crowd breathed a sigh of relief when they saw Pundit Divakaran, the local wise man who came to witness the Swami. He was learned and had traveled all over India and the Himalayas. While the Pundit observed Swami, it was Soman Pillai, the president of the Local Panchayat who queried, giving him all due respect.

"Pandit-ji, the holy man hasn't moved or had any food for days. Should we wake him from his deep meditation?" His juddering whisper disclosed his concern for the health of Swami. Dabbing his chin, he stared into the Swami's glowing face. After few long moments of contemplation, he broke the silence.

"He has to be a saint. Only a saint can live without food and water for days." He told them about the enlightened sages who could abandon their body anytime like we remove clothes. Their spirits can travel to faraway places and the body needs no food or water. He vouched that he had seen people like that while he traveled through the Himalayas, and was amazed at their powers.

~

ON THE THIRD day, they heard his voice. It was late afternoon when he opened his eyes. Most of the women had gathered round, having finished all their household chores early. The presence of a saint in their village excited everyone. Nila and her mother had also joined the crowd that day. When Nila looked to the sky as the sunset was nearing, she noticed an eagle circling, and it was at that moment Swami opened his eyes. The bird reminded her of the mysterious eagle of old who soared into the sky and escorted the procession of people who carried jewelry and precious stones from the *Pandalam* royal palace to the *Sabarimala* Temple, where the deity Lord *Ayyappa,* resided. In *Sabarimala*, the eagle would reappear at the time of the return of the jewelry to the palace. It always disappeared into the clouds when the procession reached the palace.

Swami stared at the crowd intently and scanned everyone, one at a time. Anyone who had the strength to look into his penetrating eyes, while he gazed at them, felt a spark of something flare inside them. Nila was timid, so she looked at his feet the moment he looked in her direction. She didn't feel anything, but her intuition told her he was different from any others she had ever seen before. Swami took a sip of the tender coconut water served in the coconut itself with its top of its shell chopped. He waited for another moment before taking a deep breath and nodded to convey his happiness in seeing them all. To the eagerly waiting crowd, he began to tell a story in his calming and quiet voice. Many moved forward to hear his whispers, while Nila had an advantage and a front-row view.

"There once lived a woman who led a very miserable life. Her life was so miserable that there was nothing to look forward to. She felt only despair and anxiety. All her hopes of finding happiness had withered away. She toiled from dawn to late night, engaging in household chores, taking care of her children and meeting the demands of her husband. She cooked, cleaned, and prepared meal after meal. Her children often caused trouble both in school and in the neighborhood, and she had to attend to those complaints between her life struggles. Her husband had no time to share her burden or console her. He had a job but never saved anything. She dreamed of living in the biggest house in her neighborhood, but at that time she had the smallest. She wished her husband was more caring and her children well behaved. When in reality, they were just the opposite of what she had wished for."

Swami paused for a moment to let the tale sink deep into the psyche of his listeners. Then when he was sure all had received enough time to ponder he asked, "Is there anyone here who can relate to her pain?"

Swami waited patiently with a deep smile spread across his face. The women looked at each other, and one by one they raised their hands. Soon, almost every woman had their hand raised. Many of the men had a hard time digesting the concept but they eagerly waited for the wisdom from the holy man.

Swami got up from the stone where he sat, climbed down, and walked into the crowd. They parted to one side. His steps took him toward a young mother who sat holding her screaming baby. The ear-piercing noise was disturbing everyone nearby. When Swami was near to her, she pressed the child's face against her own, but the baby yelled even more. Swami smiled at the mother and stroked the baby's forehead. The baby fell into a peaceful sleep and the mother looked fondly at Swami. It stunned everyone who was gathered and they held their palms together, close to their chests in appreciation of his divinity. After returning to his seat, Swami continued with the story.

"The woman couldn't take her miseries anymore. One morning after her husband had left for work and her children were in school, she decided to run away. She walked to the neighboring village where no one knew who she was. There she rested in a shelter in the market square. Hiding behind its wooden pillar, she gazed at the people coming and going.

On the other side of the road, she noticed a very pleasant woman selling fruits sitting on the ground. The market woman sat on a handmade wooden wheelchair. The despondent woman saw that the lady in the wheelchair was missing both her legs. Some people came near her just to chat with her. Everyone seemed to enjoy her company. Being near her made them cheery. *Unbelievable!* The woman thought to herself. *How could an amputee, one struggling to make ends meet, be so happy and be the sunshine for everyone around her?* She wondered and decided to ask the fruit-selling woman herself how she could be so joyful… She waited until there was no one near her before asking her question.

"I see you are very happy and make everyone around you feel better. I have no doubt you struggle really hard to survive. How are you able to do this?"

The fruit-selling woman just laughed aloud at her question, then queried, "I haven't seen you before, are you new here?" The village woman explained her life of misery and how she couldn't live that life anymore. When she had finished, the woman in the wheelchair who sat with heaps of apples, grapes, and pineapples around her, didn't show any emotion, but asked the village woman to join her for lunch.

That afternoon when the shops were closing for lunch, the market woman covered all her fruits with a tarpaulin sheet.

Pushing her knuckles on the ground, she lifted herself up onto the wheelchair. She signaled the village woman to follow her. She pedaled the wheelchair with her hands. It moved forward quickly and the village woman had a tough time keeping up walking behind the wheelchair. On her way, the fruit seller stopped at a street vendor to collect rice porridge in an aluminum canister that she hung on a hook on the wheelchair's edge. In a few minutes, they had reached a beaten down shack. It was tiny and had a blue thick plastic sheet on its roof to protect it from the rain. The woman got out of her cart and quickly hopped inside just using her hands with the food in her lap. The village woman followed her inside. There she saw a paralyzed man and a blind child sat beside him.

"He was born blind. When I was carrying him, we met with an accident. The auto-rickshaw we were riding was crushed by a bus which left my husband paralyzed, and I lost both my legs." But instead of her face showing pain it showed only pure love. The woman shuffled over to her family and, using her hands, fed her family the rice porridge. In the dim light, the village woman saw the bright smile on all their faces.

"We all could have been dead. We are not perfect, yet we are here for each other. We are happy the way we are and grateful we still have one another." She continued to feed her loved ones until, eventually, she looked at the village woman and continued, "Happiness and sorrow is a filter we have created inside us to hide the realities. To begin with, we are fortunate to be in this world… even if for a short time. Is it worth spending our precious lives in misery and tears?"

Tears rolled down the village woman's cheeks, but it wasn't out of sadness but of joy, for finding the true meaning of happiness herself.

"Thank you!" She didn't wait for the reply. She couldn't wait to reach home before everyone returned.

Swami concluded his story and stood before addressing the crowd, "So, now you know where to find true happiness. Don't let greed, our selfishness, and ego ever blind us from finding it."

⌒〜

IN THE FOLLOWING days, Swami taught the women lessons that changed the way they looked at life and everything around them. Women of the village were enlightened by the power of managing time. They used the spare time to organize and streamline their chores for enriching themselves. Nila was amazed how it slowly changed village life. Women buried deep under the household chores began to see a world of opportunities, which they never believed they had access to. A world where they felt like onlookers, suddenly they were pulled onto center stage. It let them dream and gave fuel to break socially-imposed norms. They learned about prioritizing tasks and planning them to apply in real life. They took on the responsibility of money management and budgeting in their households. In their leisure time, women discussed their power. They purchased their groceries from the wholesalers and sold their produces without middlemen. Women joined hands to begin a startup business in catering services and delivered food to homes and weddings. More than anything, Swami taught them to be positive and focus on the strength that exists in everyone.

One thing that impressed Nila even more was Swami's answer when someone in the crowd asked why there were plenty of religions teaching love but the world was having a hard time getting along.

He answered, "Until you place an honest effort to build a personal relationship with God, religions can only serve as a social guild. When you succeed, you will experience His presence in everyone and begin to love one another."

A WEEK HAD passed since Swami's arrival. It was a Sunday evening; a large crowd had gathered around him. They all waited patiently for his wisdom. He began with an assertion.

"Why are we given this life?

Why were you chosen to be in this world?

You didn't choose the time of your birth or death

So who could have predicted them accurately?

We come to fulfill a purpose

There is a purpose behind every step we take.

A purpose for our life was already written even before we were born

You are dear to me like the flower bud loves the nightfall

Like the sunshine that erases the shadow of darkness."

He then narrated the story of a lost man. "There was a man who had lost everything and ended up in a village that had a heart with every shade of selflessness. Its air held the scent of jasmine and the cheer of marigold. They fed him when he was hungry, they gave him a place to live, and found him a job within a school to survive. He was the janitor who helped the local tutorial college where high school and college kids came for tuition and supplemental education. Students loved him; he always rang the bell a few minutes early and made the breaks a bit longer. He brought tea for the instructors from the nearby tea stall. Between his tasks, everyone thought he was daydreaming, sitting on the half-wall outside the classrooms. Instead, he educated himself by listening to Shakespeare from the literature classroom and watched the students solve algebra and calculus problems. At night, he read books that the students left in the classrooms, and worked on the unsolved problems on the blackboard. He helped the ones who couldn't quite grasp the learning and taught them tricks to comprehend quickly. He used stories and the power of images to the ones that couldn't remember. When it came to a time to find a replacement for the lead teacher, Raman Menon, who moved to Northern Kerala, they looked no further than their caretaker to take the role. The resident caretaker was confident enough to be the interim teacher, and the students exuberantly welcomed the idea.

He surprised everyone. Learning became a joyous experience, and the burdens that came along became lighter and lighter as time progressed. He transformed the campus environment to feel like an ancient *Gurukula,* an ashram for learning that circled around the Guru. Teachers became devoted to their students and catered to each individual's learning style. The students showed more commitment and sincerity to attain knowledge. Students from other nearby towns rushed to join them. That year the institute's students had a hundred percent pass on the university exams with a few of the students receiving honors. That had been unheard in the school's history, and it continued its growth as an institution of excellence.

One day the caretaker/interim teacher doused everyone in sadness when he announced he was leaving the school to follow his true calling. He left one morning without anyone knowing and he started his new path, rambling through every shrine and climbed all the holy mountains in the country. At the end of his journey, he halted at the holy *Badrinath* in the lap of the Himalayan mountains. He meditated sitting on the shores of the *Alaknanda River,* overlooking the snow-covered mountains. He continued his pilgrimage for many years until he experienced the unrelenting light that filled his soul."

Swami finished his tale, closed his eyes, and fell into meditation.

"Swami is our Balan Mash. The holy one is our Balan Mash." People began with a murmur until it became a reverberating chant that charged every particle inside the boundaries. Eventually the whole gathering came to silence after they digested who Swami really was. They waited till it was dark before dispersing to their beds, each one promising to join their beloved Swami the next day.

But the following morning, the news of Swami's disappearance shook the whole village. The news spread quickly. Anxious, everyone gathered around the stone and the Neem tree at the edge of the hill where Swami had sat. Swami had left a palm-leaf manuscript on the stone. Divakaran Pundit picked it up and browsed it quickly, then raised his hand signaling everyone to be silent and read it for all to listen.

Let me share a prayer for you, my people.

Let my soul rejoice in your realm
Let me never forget you live within
You blew life into my breath
You strummed a rhythm for my heart to beat
A dust saved from the wind
You are the mountain; I cling to you
Lost rain drop yearning for the seas
Oh grace, I long for you
I submit myself
Flood me with your light to see goodness
Lighten my burden to lend my shoulders
Ebb away my pride to make peace
Help me to silence myself to hear your voice
And I pray...
May your light lead my way
May your wisdom adorn my tongue
May your power shield me
May your love be the reason for my joy

It took a few days for the villagers to get over the Swami's departure. But they all overcame the blues quickly and were extremely gratified that he had graced them with his presence, even if it had been for a short time. The wisdom Swami rained over them stayed with them, and they never forgot the secret of happiness. The Neem grew into a giant tree. Under it, there always sat a few villagers, contemplating and reciting the prayer he had taught them.

A new life. No more lonely
Beginning of volunteer work
at the hospital

We never knew
Flowers could see.
They feel.
They dream.
Their shy eyes we never see.
They never err.
Bloom in the lonely darkness
Exhaling its joy.

Never fear darkness.
Even in the thickest night
We find our way.
Our hidden eye color blind.
Pupil never needs to dilate.
It sees the light beyond darkness.
When we begin to believe in it
It will come to us.

Living among the Life Savers

Maybe you know them,
Or you may have heard or read about them
Or it may be you
A collection of inspiring anecdotes from the lives of ordinary
people with extraordinary courage.

Apparition

I T WAS KAMALA who had told Nila to try volunteering at the local hospital when she expressed an interest in doing something to escape from her besetting boredom. Kamala, a family friend was in her final year of residency at the University Hospital, and was always encouraging Nila to pursue a career in the healthcare arena. She believed it would keep Nila busy, but could also help her identify a career path in the healthcare industry.

"Blood... I cannot stomach the sight of it," Nila responded with disgust when the topic came up for the first time a few months ago. But, Kamala had a persuasive nature and talked Nila out of her fears by helping to get her to relate.

"Imagine your father or mother were bleeding from a fatal injury, do you pass out or try to help them?"

"I would certainly help them," Nila snapped.

Kamala smiled gently and rested a comforting hand on Nila's shoulder. "You said it, Nila, I used to be like you. If you are afraid of something, that fear is not helping anyone; it hurts everyone and makes you weak. Don't let the fear stop you from living your life purpose. When someone is hurt, nothing should be occupying your mind other than to save a life or help to ease their pain." Kamala paused for a moment and continued. "In the ER, when I see a person covered in blood or struggling to breathe, I tell myself, this is someone dear to me, and my fear leaves my body and doesn't come back."

Nila spent some time mulling over Kamala's words and when she felt comfortable, she began her volunteer work. By then fall had begun and she found that the rest of the city was a little blue as the impending harsh winter was upon them. Nila was eager, although she didn't wish any pain or illness among her people; she wanted to care for them. She wanted to share her joy and spend time with them to make her presence soothe their groggy minds.

The hospital staff was impressed by the energy and commitment Nila displayed when she was around. The volunteer coordinator rotated her through different departments and gave her access to most areas in the hospital. Nila found the ER the most frightening, but she held on to its pace and changing faces without being absorbed by its insanity and negativity. She learned to take patients' vital signs and perform CPR. She became used to the blood, screams, and cops who became a familiar fixture in the ER. But the one thing that brought Nila to tears were the several miraculous feats by the medical staff who brought near-death patients back to life. She learned to stay cool and calm in all situations, even when her heart felt like it was beating out of her chest. It was all overwhelming but she comforted the patients who had experienced extreme trauma and swallowed her own fear and she held the patients' hands as she watched surgeries, including brain and open-heart operations.

Patience, patience, patience… she would repeat to herself when things troubled her. She overcame her flaws by dressing wounds, feeding patients, and listening to their murmurs of distress. She was totally surprised by the number of patients who ended up in the ER doing ludicrous things. One young man came in almost dead, bleeding out because he had been playing the knife game where one tries to poke a pencil in between the fingers as fast as one can, but he had used a sharp knife.

Then one day Nila found a way to be herself. She began to help at the hospital gift shop delivering flowers and gifts to patients. Sometimes it was helping people who found themselves lost on the many different floors in the hospital. In the hallways, she came face to face with human beings who were showing their true and raw feelings rather than the usual ego and pride. When people were in pain, whether it be actual or the pain of seeing a loved one in a serious condition, Nila witnessed true vulnerability. At the hospital beds, she sat with the lonely ones listening to their struggles to accept their failures, which hurt more than the pain their ailment inflicted. She listened to them; she sat with them until she could bring a little cheer to their deeply wrinkled face, or transcend the bitterness into a glimmer of joy. She was like a bright shaft of early morning light that came at odd hours for them, or at a time when they really wanted someone near.

One day while she was returning after delivering flowers at the newborn center, she stopped at the nursery for a moment. Through the glass window, she looked at the sleeping babies in their tiny cribs tucked in pink and blue blankets. She imagined herself holding one of them and singing lullabies. Her vision blurred as her thoughts drifted to the memories of the countless miscarriages she had struggled with over the years.

"Hey you…taking a break?" Mrs. Johnson, an aid at the nursery, came out to greet her chortling. Nila quickly wiped her eyes and hid the tears that dripped through her fingers. Then answered with a smile, avoiding eye contact to hide her glistening eyes from her.

"What's happened, Nila, you seem to be not in your normal cheerful mood? Are you alright, girl?"

"Oh, Mrs. Johnson, I am perfectly alright. I was just looking at the babies. Aren't they adorable?" Nila responded, but she couldn't control her words that were threatening to expose her sorrow.

"Come inside," Mrs. Johnson placed a comforting arm around Nila's shoulders. "Let me tell you a story so you can be yourself again."

Nila followed her but was a bit nervous as she knew the story would have something to do with her gloom. She sat next to Mrs. Johnson where both had a good view of the newborns. The room had controls and monitors that could be zoomed on babies that needed special attention.

Mrs. Johnson's full name was Maggi Johnson, and she was a volunteer like Nila. She had lost her entire family in a horrible car accident a few years ago. Her husband had been driving their nineteen-year-old twin daughters off to college after Christmas break. Their car slipped on black ice and rear-ended a gas tanker. The collision had sent the car out of control and into the center median, which caused another collision. Maggi's daughters had died on the spot, and her husband lost both his legs, but in a month, an infection from his injury cost him his life, too.

"In a few weeks, the families and friends faded away leaving a vacuum in me," Maggi continued. "Loneliness and the grief were almost impossible to handle." Her voice cracked with emotion. "I started to withdraw into myself. Every time I heard a child's laugh, I would close the windows and go into a room in the back of the house. I went away on Halloween to avoid kids knocking at the door. Some days the grief was so hard to carry, suicide felt like the only option. But, I decided I would stay alive to make my life meaningful. I couldn't let the deaths of my family stop me from fulfilling my reason for being on this earth. I held onto my shield of faith and strength. One night while I was deep in sleep, I was awakened by an intense cry of a baby outside. A cry that reminded me of my twins when they were born. I ran down the stairs and looked around, thinking someone had abandoned their newborn at my doorsteps. But there was no one there and no child.

I continued to hear the crying again and again for several nights. But each time I went to look, I found no child or anyone there. One day while returning from visiting a friend at the hospital, I passed through the nursery lobby and heard the same cry from a stroller that had just passed me by. I stood still for a moment, as I couldn't control my pounding heart and I found myself a little dizzy. After that, I began to believe that my loved ones had returned to this world as little bundles of joy for someone else. Angels born into this world as babies again. I knew for sure, I will never know which babies they reincarnated into or where they are, but I feel so good knowing that they exist somewhere near or far from me," Maggi smiled to herself and patted down her skirt.

"You see, Nila, life is a precious gift to us for a limited time. Why make it miserable? Every negative emotion is in our head. I volunteer at many different hospitals in their neonatal centers as I feel I have a bond with every baby born in this world. I also run a website where I give comfort and advice to anyone going through catastrophes in their lives and need someone to hold on to. It doesn't take much to leave a lasting imprint on another person's soul. I hope that my own awful experience had a reason and that reason is, I am meant to help as many other people live their own difficult path."

Nila left the nursery feeling a mix of emotions from sadness to enlightenment. Maggi's life story had stirred something deep inside of her. Something that she knew would lead to what her purpose was for her own life. While coming out from the nursery, Nila felt like a breeze out of a rosebud, flowing light and smooth to touch the silky wings of a monarch.

Raising the Dead

THROUGHOUT HER LIFE, Nila had never been part of the workforce, and the hospital environment scared her more. For this reason, she felt extremely nervous during the initial days of her volunteer work at the hospital. She would keep her eyes peeled for a familiar or a friendly face over the hallways, often peeking at the nurse's stations whenever she passed by one. Everyone looked too busy, though. She wondered why they never had a moment to spare, even to flash a smile at the people passing by.

It was at the end of her second week of working, when Nila was walking towards her car that she noticed a girl in nurse's scrubs who looked like she was from India. In the excitement of seeing someone who looked to be from her home country, Nila got the nurse's attention by waving and yelling, "Hello." Nila was pretty sure she got her attention, but the person got in her car and drove away ignoring Nila's presence.

The following week, Nila saw her again in the cafeteria. Nila was looking for a vacant seat to eat in the crowded dining area during the busy lunch hour. She recognized the girl from the parking lot having lunch and sitting alone in a corner. Nila walked toward her, greeted her, and introduced herself before sitting down. Nila snuck a look at the nurse's name tag which read 'Neena Philip R.N'. But Neena didn't express even a fraction of excitement as Nila had of meeting a fellow countryman. In fact, she seemed a bit hesitant to respond to the conversations Nila was attempting to instigate. Instead, the woman reacted impassively and rather quietly. Neena quickly ate her lunch and left saying she was running late and offered to catch up with Nila later. Nila was disappointed in her frostiness. She wondered if there was something wrong with Neena that could explain why she was avoiding Nila.

~

A FEW WEEKS had passed and it was on a Sunday afternoon when Nila and Ashok, ran into Neena while at the mall. Seeing Nila on the other side of the mall, Neena came running toward her. Neena's husband and two small children followed her at a normal pace. What a sudden change in a moody woman who ignored her like a stranger, Nila wondered. When her husband and kids caught up with her, she introduced them.

"Nila, meet my family, they arrived from India last week."

"That is fabulous!" Nila responded, encouraging her to continue talking as she was still in shock that Neena was talking to her at all.

She continued, "I am so… sorry for not spending much time with you at work. Did you feel I was rude? You wouldn't believe how much stress I was going through."

"That's ok. I am so glad to see you again, and that you now have your family with you," Nila replied.

While the husbands were introducing themselves, Nila invited them to have a coffee and they continued the conversation.

"Prior to joining the hospital two months ago, I was in

California." Nila listened to Neena, and the ordeal she went through before she came to Minneapolis. Nila was upset and wondered how such things could happen in a country where laws are enforced justly, and it is impossible to ignore them.

In California, she was literally enslaved by an unscrupulous nursing recruiter who helped her to migrate to this country. Neena came with a Green Card status through a program that allowed recruiters and hospitals to bring foreign-educated nurses into the country. It was intended to tackle the nursing shortages in the country. Neena was promised a full-time job in a hospital with excellent pay and benefits. In return, the owner of the company made her pay a hefty amount, which he said was to cover the visa fees, airline tickets, and to help her find a nursing job. Prior to arrival, Neena had to sign contracts that committed her to an exclusive relationship with the recruiter, with high penalty fees for breaching the contract. For Neena, she had no choice but to sign the papers or lose an opportunity to gain a better life and career.

Neena's recruiter, Sikander, strongly suggested she come first, and have the rest of her family join later once she was settled. Once Neena arrived in the US, she came to know about Sikander's several small businesses, including a travel agency and a restaurant. Immediately after her arrival, he tactfully confiscated her passport and forced her to live in the back room of his small travel agency office. He had her work from open to close at the agency for free lodging and the awful leftover food that he brought from home. Some days, Sikander let Neena have the leftover Chinese food he bought for his lunch. He also limited Neena's ability to contact her family in India; he locked the international calling facility on the office phone and monitored her calls when he was around.

Once every few days, Sikander's wife took Neena home with her, where she made Neena do the household cleaning and cooking for them. There she ate fresh food and took a hot shower before she left to her den. Within a month, Sikander found her a temporary job at a nursing home. He paid her in cash; just a tiny fraction of what she was being billed. He promised Neena she would be paid the rest when her family arrived. When she asked about the other nurses who had come to this country with her, Sikander was furious and rained down on her with verbal abuse. Neena never asked about them again. Especially when he also threatened to cancel her family's visa if she didn't work for him for the five years mentioned in the contract.

By the time eight months had passed, working for almost nothing, Neena feared she would never see an end to this. She gathered the courage to talk about her situation to one of her colleagues, Nancy, at the nursing home. Nancy and her husband helped Neena to find her present job in Minneapolis. They assisted her in fleeing California to escape the modern-day slavery that was going unnoticed. Even after coming to the new place, she feared retaliation from the recruiter.

Nila was enraged as she listened to Neena's story.

"No one should take advantage of people's situation. No one should live in fear when the laws are written to protect them."

Neena motivated everyone to do something to avoid this happening to anyone else. Before they parted that day, they all decided to contact the nursing advocacy groups and the federal agencies as the first step. Maybe it was a small move, but it was a good beginning, they thought.

Snakes and Ladder

VOLUNTEERING AT THE hospital was a way for Nila to escape her boredom and loneliness, but even there, where she sought solace and meaning, she was besieged by lonely people. The old wanted to talk and be listened to by someone they felt comfortable with. So, Nila made a point to stop and chat with the ones who looked forward to her visit while she idled through the hallway.

Volunteer work became more exciting for her when she was asked to assist Dr. Bush with some research work he was part of. It focused on the relationship between a patient's moods versus speed of recovery. She was assigned a few patients who were lonely, and had been in care for a long time. Being lonely herself, it was easy for her to transform into an unassuming role. But being the talkative kind of girl that she was, she struggled to be an ardent listener. She reminded herself to be patient and put a lid on her compulsive mouth to avoid interrupting. Through the many stories Nila listened to, she was rather alarmed to learn about the loneliness people go through, especially when they get older. Back home in India, this kind of loneliness never occurred because everyone lived under the same roof as joint families. The old were always respected and taken care of, their wisdom and life experience were always given precedence.

Nila continued her research for Dr. Bush and heard many stories. When they were finished, she would entertain them with adventures and chivalries from her childhood. If she had multiple listeners, she brightened their mood by personifying her fantasy characters, enacting them with her talent to impersonate animals and famous people.

One of Nila's biggest fans was Rebecca, a ninety-two year old woman who had outlived all her six children. She was a workhorse that never paused until her hip didn't want to move as fast as her legs wanted her to. Her story was inspiring; a journey of an ordinary housewife married to the head of a major corporation. Rebecca's husband died when she was forty, leaving her with six children and nothing much for them to hold on to. Life was a torn cloud thrown into the storm, struggling to float onto an edge. Somehow, she mustered up the courage to overcome her misfortune and she began to fight back, without crying over her misfortune. Thereafter, she never looked back.

Rebecca opened a small soup and sandwich place on a street corner, with homemade bread and the soup recipe her grandma had shared with her. Its unique flavor and addicting taste made her tiny store famous all around her town. Soon she had customers flocking to her shop from nearby towns, and traveling salesmen coming through. They all wanted her soup and sandwiches. And each customer would impart advice and guidance on how to develop as a business owner and she grew her little shop into a successful franchise. In a few years, it grew to several hundred shops all over the country. She had even been on the cover of coveted magazines, and several articles were published about her success story all around the globe.

Even when she hit her eighties, she was healthy and never bothered to retire or take it easy. She traveled all over the country, running her many businesses. But her slump began when she was visiting one of her stores; she slipped on the wet floor injuring herself so badly she had to have knee and hip replacement surgery. It didn't go well, and she never really recovered. After months of hospitalization, she was moved to an assisted care facility where her health deteriorated even more. Somewhere along the way, she lost her courage and zeal to live and felt she was on the last leg of her life. What really hurt her was, everyone she cared about never wanted to spend time with her except on special occasions, like Thanksgiving or the 4th of July. She didn't blame them though; she knew they were busy with their own lives. Still, it was heartbreaking to go from one who had everything in a life filled with friends and associates to a single, lonely room. A time… that she hoped everyone would be around her.

"I was always healthy and feared nothing," Rebecca explained to Nila one day. "I had never been to a hospital for treatment, and always had people around me at my command. Now you see how helpless I am and vulnerable I have become."

Nila felt sorry for Rebecca, who had become her idol and inspiration. It made her think, that all it could take was a wrong turn and in a split second, even the most glorious person can hit the dust and feel worthless. She prayed to be humbler than ever and burn down all her ego in that warmth. Nila consoled Rebecca with a warm hug.

"You are such a blessing young lady, thank you for being here for me." Rebecca patted Nila's arms like a little girl and pinched her on her cheeks with her bony fingers. They both burst into laughter, dissolving all regrets.

～

REBECCA WAS JUST one of many she tended to; there were many she met during her volunteer work. Spending time and getting to know the people created an interest in her to learn more about the human mind. She pondered and realized that many people were placing their happiness on materialistic things rather than embracing life and enjoying their time on this earth. Nila helped the patients cultivate a positive outlook on life. Through experimenting with increased physical activities, meditation, and laughing she experienced firsthand how patient's moods could be improved so they recover more quickly with less pain to bear.

Rose Garden

NILA MET SOME truly remarkable people on her journey of self-discovery, but one lady named Susan Anderson transformed Nila's outlook on confronting life's undesirable realities. Susan was a stay-at-home mother of four children. She taught Nila how to look at life's perturbing events, to face its miseries by convincing ourselves to live believing every moment of life is a blessing. Nila realized that inspiring moments happen everywhere and every day. But most times we fail to notice them because our eyes are blinded by things we perceive as being more important. Our eyes and ears focus only on our own little world. We immerse ourselves in worries that really only exist in our own minds. And when we truly experience such good deeds through the life of ordinary people, our heart raises our spirit into a searching mode. We look for possibilities to be like them.

Susan was a tall, confident woman. Her black hair with a splattering of gray gave her an elegant look. With a never-fading smile on her face and the large, round bifocal glasses that hung by a chain around her neck, it was impossible to forget her even with just one visit. Nila thought a positive vibe existed in Susan, and it transformed into a good feeling for all who interacted with her.

Nila met Susan at the hospital when Drew, the youngest of

Susan's children, was admitted for treatment. In her volunteer position at the hospital, Nila had spent quite a bit of time assisting and giving company to Susan. Susan's son had an extreme case of cerebral palsy. To make matters worse, he had a rare condition that gave him hives and breathing problems due to allergies. This made trips to the emergency room a regular thing and it nearly always ended in a prolonged hospital stay.

Her son Drew was diagnosed with the disease in his first year of life. Susan immediately left her teaching job to take care of him. She was his full-time caregiver and never regretted her decision to stop working. She felt it a rewarding journey of parenting inundated with unconditional love.

"It's been a long journey—but I've reached the point where I feel blessed instead of hurt," Susan told her story one day while Nila was at the hospital.

"I thank the Lord every day for giving me my child."

Really? Nila wanted to ask, but she controlled herself. But surprising Nila, Susan continued as if she had read her mind. "Unless you experience them, you wouldn't see the little miracles that God does in our life every day through him. He has a reason. A purpose for displaying his work over us. By choosing us for Drew, he emptied us to fill us with his unceasing compassion."

~

THEY NOTICED DREW couldn't sit up or crawl or do anything like his siblings did when they were at that age. They knew something was wrong but didn't want to accept it. The words Cerebral Palsy came as a shock to them.

"Please, please... Oh God, not my baby. This isn't happening to us. Please—not my kid!"

The doctor kept on talking but they were numb, and their

hearts were still. Reality eventually sunk in with a thousand unanswered questions over what fate had gifted them.

For months, Susan pulled away from everyone, sitting on her balcony for long hours gazing into the emptiness, angry and frustrated in guilt. Their marriage suffered, but her husband was very supportive and was with her to overcome the toughest time of their life. But in a few months Drew began to respond to them with the most beautiful smile she had ever seen. He seemed to understand a lot of what they were saying and babbled at them like a two-month-old.

"We all fell in love with him more than ever," Susan explained. Drew's disabilities never bothered them again, and they all felt that he was perfect in his own way. They couldn't imagine him any other way. They learned to love him for who he was. Their minds learned to enjoy his beautiful moments, rather than focusing on the hurt they had initially felt when Drew was diagnosed.

Drew's brothers and sisters treated him the same as they would any other child. They learned patience and to respect everyone's differences. They helped other special needs children, and were never hesitant to be with them and were never afraid of getting close to them.

After several years, the commitment and perseverance of this loving mother and her supportive family started to pay off. A child who could just babble for several years, now at thirteen, could speak two dozen words. He got about by using an electric wheelchair that he used for long distances and a walker for shorter ones. Susan prayed every day that there would be more innovations in the treatment of children affected by cerebral palsy. She was confident that one day her son would be ready to take on the world by himself without her help. And if her life wasn't hard enough looking after Drew and his siblings, she was involved in organizing events for families with disabilities. Her goal was to make every one of them feel they are part of one big family. Nila believed, whoever it was, everyone she had met in life never failed to impart a positive outlook within her. She felt, almost always, that her eyes saw what they wanted to see, and looked away from everything her mind avoided... though her heart told something else. Travelling like a tiny bubble for a moment through a glimpse Susan's world caused her to live in the moment, appreciating its beauty and listening to her humming heart.

Precious Moments

NILA HAD NEVER seen a truc fighter in her life until she met Silvia Rogers, a brave woman who had been diagnosed with terminal cancer. Silvia described her own situation as living on bonus time gifted from God. She had been expected to only live a few months but had survived more than a year so far. She had an attitude that nothing could beat her, even the pain that radiated through her bones. Nila grew close to Silvia while she was in the hospital for pain management therapy. Nila would stop by Silvia's room whenever she found the time. She felt so connected to the woman and badly wanted to soothe her pain in every way she could. Nila learned about Silvia's journey through agony and the way she got through the pain to find the strength to help others like herself. People had nothing to look forward to but the fearful moment that would carry them away to the afterlife. Silvia motivated them to feel like the dew drops that become diamond dust in the morning sunlight.

Even in her struggles and fight for life in pain, Silvia never lost the charm on her face or her pleasing attitude. The more she learned about her, the more Nila's admiration grew and wanted to be like her. She wondered how someone like Silvia had handled the news of her diagnosis. Nila wanted to hear from her. One day while tending to Silvia, she thought of bringing up it. She was hesitant, still she brought it up in the conversation.

"I know, Silvia, it is hard, but I wonder…" Nila felt awkward and paused for a moment

"Come on, Nila… we are pals, you can ask me anything, my dear." Silvia wanted to help her feel free.

"How did you… how did you find out you were sick… with cancer?" Nila blushed.

"Oh… that is not something you need to be embarrassed to ask." Silvia looked deep into Nila's eyes. "I was twenty-seven when I was diagnosed with breast cancer. It was while on a hiking trip in Colorado when a severe pain spiraled through my left chest while climbing. When I touched it, it felt like a sharp hook stuck in my heart, someone ruthlessly pulling at me. A few days after the biopsy, I was told I have cancer." Nila sat next to her, listening. Her heart was pounding hard but she kept staring at the small whiteboard that said, 'Nurse on Duty: Denise Williams'.

"Hearing the word cancer, I screamed and jumped from the seat. My initial reaction was not to believe it; I was terrified of the thought of having cancer. The following moments of silence were the most excruciating. I hoped to disappear, and just be a memory in someone's mind that was never there. After going through several cycles of chemotherapy, I was totally wrecked. I hated the hallucinations the chemo gave. The changes it made to my body… turning me into a different person… someone with a distorted mind, even after the illness completely left me." She could feel Silvia's voice cracking. To comfort the valiant woman, she stretched her arm to soothe her shoulders.

After a few treatment sessions and few months' remission, she felt like life was returning to normalcy. Her hair grew back and she began to look at herself as before. She started enjoying life again and felt confident to take back control over her life.

For her, it felt so different getting back to her routine after being removed from life's sequence for so long. She approached life, and the moments it gave, as a gift to be enjoyed. She sat breathing the freshness of the cool breeze after the rain. A rainbow and the clear sky looked more beautiful than ever. She woke up to listening to the robins and sparrows, watched them building nests, their quarrels and smooches through the kitchen window. At night she watched stars, and even in the darkest nights, she kept staring into its depths. Soon she began to see tiny diamonds appearing and eventually stars filled the sky. It motivated her to the fullest. Soon she continued with her career, spending time with her friends and giving herself new goals to achieve, reflected by her new outlook on life. She never felt such inundated joy in her life and the sweetness spilled into the air that surrounded her.

Silvia took a vow never to think of cancer again or to even believe it could hit her again. But the quiescent sky swayed again thinning the layer of air that surrounded her, protecting from the past. Silvia was celebrating Christmas with her nieces and nephews at her parents' house. While she was unwrapping the presents, she felt a stabbing pain in her breast. It repeated and then she felt her breast and there was a lump.

"How could this be true?" She couldn't breathe, and she feared her veins would burst. The intense pressure building within her skull felt like she was being crushed in a giant wrench. But this time the news of the cancer was worse than the last. She was diagnosed with secondary stage four cancer which had spread to her lymph nodes. By this point, the tumor had found its way into her lungs and heart. She was given between two and five months to live. Her world came crashing down once again.

Chemotherapy continued, and the illness was responding positively to the treatment. This news kept her hopes alive. It turns out that the fear of getting sick is far worse than getting sick. The paranoia it creates makes one lose the faith, but Silvia was determined to live every moment she had left to the fullest.

Her friends suggested making a bucket list of all things she always wanted to do. Silvia gave it some thought but she didn't want a list of dreams that could never be reached. Instead, she wanted to do things that would inspire and give hope to patients like herself and people around them. She dreamed of building a beautiful castle that reached the sky. The meadow which the castle overlooked was filled with butterflies and dragonflies. In the middle of the night, when everyone was fast asleep and dreaming, she wanted to go to that magical land as a fairy, with her magic wand making all dreams come true.

Between the treatment cycles, Silvia made a few trips to the ocean to experience its vastness and feel the fine, white sand between her toes. There she also felt the frailty of human life and its transience in the universe. Even in her pain, she appreciated the beautiful gift of life from the Creator. She wondered why everyone was forced to forget to live in the moment, and instead be swallowed up by problems that are created and merely exist in their minds. She let her thoughts disappear into tiny bubbles that burst over the sand. Sometimes she sat on a protruding rock that reached into the ocean and watched the waves crash onto the shore. She felt each wave was trying to tell her something. They kept coming back again and again, but she could never under-stand their language. Maybe they understood all the frustrations from the beginning of the world and knew how to soothe and console agonizing minds. Gentle misting of sea air, feathery waves and the beauty of the setting sun against the scarlet clouds made her truly alive again. She wished to freeze those moments in the conch shell that she picked up from the sand.

She didn't need a bucket list, she enjoyed being around people whom she loved; that was how dreams come true.

Silvia believed she had the best life ever and could die content at any moment. Even whilst she endured agonizing pain, she never wanted to let her smile leave her face, and she made sure people around her were always elated in her presence. Everyone began to notice and enjoyed Silvia's sense of humor that became sharper ever since she was diagnosed. Maybe that was the way her mind was reacting to the new phase in her life. Silvia found humor in everything that she saw and experienced. She even found ways to make people laugh about her prognosis. The stories she told were all real-life experiences. She started giving inspirational talks with humor added at local support groups and made videos of them for social media. She had a large fan base that included people with terminal illnesses and their families.

It was few weeks before she died that Silvia became extremely weak, but she still found the strength to scramble through her belongings to pull out a sheet of paper with scribbled notes on it. Extending it to Nila, she said "…some thoughts I learned in my life. See what you think." Nila's eyes were blurred with tears and she couldn't read it in that moment. Later, when Nila heard about Silvia's death, she remembered the note. She quickly rifled it out of her handbag. She was overwhelmed with emotion. She felt those beautiful cursive letters were rising like grape vines to wipe her tears. While a solemn spring breeze tried to steal the paper out of her hand, she read it with her heart soaked in love for her hero.

How fortunate are we to be in this world even if
It is for a moment, or a thousand years
Rich or poor we have beaten every odd to make it this far
Why fight the wind? Let us rest till it comes on our way
Distance traveled is behind, and we never know what remains
Every moment gone brings us closer to where we belong

Why your eyes downcast when burden is just a myth
You are a child crying by the sand castle
Washed away into the ocean
Diamond born to darkness glow in the light
Beauty of roses enjoyed only in the sunlight but
The jasmine holds its breath for the night

Why do little things bother us when we grow old?
Why do we waver in fear when
We have done wonders
Bamboo grow humble as it grows taller
Thunderous storm always brings a clear sky
Let us save tears for joyous moments

Let your heart never feel lonely; it's your only friend forever
Why the weakness worries you when your strength is
unmatched
Believe in yourself; it will lift you up from any depths
You own your dreams, don't let someone control it
Not every challenge needs to be conquered
Focus on the ones dear to you

Beneath the anthill every creature is unique
Why measure everyone with the same gauge
Love is a beautiful gift; let it never be unlit
In the rush make time to see butterflies hovering
Over the wildflowers, and sunrise over the misty hills
Listen to the chickadees sing, and breathe in the lilac and
the sage

Have you seen a full moon trapped in the horizon while
The sun kissed the ocean
If I could freeze time
I will find a moment when our eyes are the brightest
And the air filled with laughter spilling
With all our love for everyone around us

Who is Nila?

I F YOU ARE wondering who Nila is or who she is to me, I have no simple answer. I met her through the lines scribbled on a journal left on a park bench one summer afternoon. Did she leave it on purpose for me to find? I'll never know... maybe it was fate, that it is destined for something beyond what she could handle.

In my journey through those immersing pages, I wandered through her mind which never seemed to rest. I traveled wherever it took me. I learned a lot about her, in fact, perhaps more than anyone who knew her and maybe even more than she knew herself.

Some of those pages carried the scent of jasmine and roses. When I closed my eyes, I could smell the same flower she breathed and felt them blooming all around me. Some of the words she wrote were blurred. Circles of tears had made tiny dents in the paper. I tried to be like her, to see the faces she saw, to listen to the voices she heard. Some pages never wanted to be turned and I would stare at them for hours before I could move on. Along with her childhood memories, Nila had kept a dry banyan tree leaf, and a tiny piece of a peacock feather. She would dream and wish that the feather would split into two and then keep multiplying. The beauty becoming a part of her.

Caricatures in the margins were of real people that came alive in my sleep. I could feel their presence, but they always disappeared before I opened my eyes. I'll never know if one of them was Nila. If I knew how she looked, I would have tried my best to find her, to return her to the journal.

I don't remember at which point she began to intrude into my life… it was like we shared the same soul. I started to see the world she wrote about. I saw the face of Neelan on the street corners, and near the grocery stores. They all had the same intense eyes. Some of them had "help wanted" signs across their chests. I felt they all wanted to tell me their stories. I saw Joseph Muthalali and Public Prosecutor Advocate Sivadasan in the crowd. I didn't wait for them to talk to me. I was like the police constable Bhaskaran Nair, always impassive. I stared at them and went on my way, ignoring the music resonating from the streets of Kaipuzha.

Like Nila with her dreams, my mind gathered the strength to look beyond tragedies, piecing together positive experiences to enable me to move on. I learned to look at the ordinary lives rather than idolizing superhumans with extraordinary experiences. I wondered why we humans forget to reinvent ourselves every so often, vindicating our mind by blaming fate which influences our destiny.

I walked through the busy farmers market eating irresistible pickles, breathing the freshly cut roses and touching the farm fresh vegetables. I tried to connect the dots, trying to live through the unknowns to find its meaning. I went back to the innocence of childhood with Maloo and Ravi. I felt feeble in my existence watching the tragically short lives of Fatima and Jamal.

Through Nila's eyes, I saw the abused Shahana and later the disabled fruit vendor who struggled to feed her ailing family. I found an answer to the reason why we all see things differently, even when we look through the same window. I learned to search the faces and perplexed smiles to find what boils within them.

Fears tamed… dice rolled for a chance to change fate hoping for a better life. Dreams of a bold woman, her longing for freedom in a life compromised through an arranged marriage.

Some days when looking in the mirror, I see the reflection of Dr. Thomas Thomas. He taught me to think positively, to experience a better outcome in life; emphasizing that everything happens for a reason, and eventually everything results in something better. Other days, I saw Swami go from being a homeless man to teacher and then to an enlightened being. Swami let the soul of the village crave for a journey into happiness and self-realization.

By living among the life savers, Nila let us seek the meaning of our own life. Maybe that is why, even when my mind is busy, my eyes keep scanning for heroes like: Susan, the mother of a young boy with cerebral palsy and Mrs. Johnson, the volunteer nurse and the terminally ill and Silvia who stayed brave in the face of death. They remind me to look at life's misfortunes as a blessing, and to enjoy every moment of this precious life we are given.

Nila is not just a sari-cladded faceless girl from South Asia. She is beyond any definition of anything that divides us. She is one amongst us and could even be a part of us all. Now that we know her, we know she cannot be separated from us. Let's give her a face… a face we love and use it to replace the fences we have created between us.

My role throughout this book was to guide you through your own journey of self-discovery and enlightenment. I hope Nila's stories changes your life for the better as it has changed mine.

Beacons of Light

It doesn't matter how bad the history was,
It shaped us, and we control today's history.

Life is easy when there is someone to follow.

Good or bad every dream is seeded from a thought when the mind was
awake.

Life is a song to compose leaving us with very little control over its lyrics.

Sometimes even a firefly can light our way in the dark.

It might be the darkest night. Keep staring into its depths and
We will begin to see tiny stars appearing and soon they will fill the sky.

When we arrive with a pre-set mind, rarely is there an agreement
But with a receptive mind, we always leave in agreement.

True prayer is the communion between the soul and its source
Everything else is a noise.

I own a brain the size of a marble,
but some days God makes it glow like the moon.
How can I walk away from his light?

When we find it's very hard to see good but too easy to find faults,
We should know it is the time to clean our mind's lenses.

We have progressed enough to cut through the boundaries of space
But we stumble again and again at the little fences we have created
around us

52715505R00118

Made in the USA
Lexington, KY
19 September 2019